Lover, Traitor

ALSO BY ANNA MITGUTSCH

In Foreign Lands

Jacob

Three Daughters

Lover,

Traitor

A JERUSALEM STORY

Anna Mitgutsch

Translated by Roslyn Theobald

METROPOLITAN BOOKS

HENRY HOLT AND COMPANY   NEW YORK

Metropolitan Books
Henry Holt and Company, Inc.
Publishers since 1866
115 West 18th Street
New York, New York 10011

Metropolitan Books is an imprint of Henry Holt and Company, Inc.

Library of Congress Cataloging-in-Publication Data
Mitgutsch, Waltraud.
    [Abschied von Jerusalem. English]
    Lover, traitor : a Jerusalem story / Anna Mitgutsch.—
1st American ed.
        p.   cm.
    ISBN 0-8050-4174-5 (alk. paper)
    I. Title.
PT2673.I77A9513   1997
833'.914—dc21   97-5472

Originally published in 1995 in Germany as *Abschied von Jerusalem* by
Rowohlt Berlin Verlag GmbH

Henry Holt books are available for special promotions and premiums.
For details contact: Director, Special Markets.

First American Edition 1997

Designed by Kate Nichols

Printed in the United States of America
All first editions are printed on acid-free paper.

10   9   8   7   6   5   4   3   2   1

Lover, Traitor

I

I walked back past the Russian Church and stopped for a moment in front of the police station. Then I went down Jaffa Road, making a conscious effort not to bolt like a criminal on the run. Once I reached the corner I turned to look behind me, but casually, as if I were just trying to orient myself. No one seemed to be following.

So I headed straight for my hotel and was overcome by relief when I reached my own room and locked the door. I peered out between the slats of the shutters to see whether anyone was standing in the street below looking up at my window.

What am I thinking? Why would anyone be following me? True, I've stayed a little longer than most tourists do. The men who hang around the Old City walls, standing in the shade waiting for tourists, I'm sure they all know me by now. I look at them out the corner of my eye when they call to me and I watch them from my rusty wrought iron balcony—how they walk by with a nonchalant swagger, pretending to be idle but always with purpose etched on their taut, focused faces as they make their way to the Arab bus station or the Jaffa Gate. The air in East Jerusalem is thick with tension. It covers the Old City like a blanket, heavier on some days than on others but never lifting completely.

Most of the people in this part of the city are Palestinian. I don't really know anyone here and in any case, I can't tell one face from another; if someone were shadowing me twenty-four hours round the clock, I still couldn't pick him out from a crowd. The men stare at me, sizing me up, but I just can't look them back in the eye. The fear that someone will recognize me drives me back to the Jewish side of the city, to West Jerusalem, where I'm treated with indifference. Nobody takes any notice; I'm just another woman out shopping. But I can't seem to keep away from the Old City, where the ironic smiles hint that my secrets are showing, out on display for everyone to scoff at.

I don't know where I belong, in East Jerusalem or West, and I don't want to make a choice. It's time for me to change hotels again. Jumping from one address to another like this will only make my case look worse, but one more day here or there won't change the fact that I'm on the run. I can't go underground and deep down I suppose I want to be caught. Why else would I keep walking past the police station?

Sooner or later, I'll have to talk about what's been going on these last few weeks. I want to be ready, to explain how it started, to have good reasons for what I did and convincing answers for the questions they might throw at me. It'll all depend on how I present the information—how skillfully I stretch the things I will tell them to cover up the gaps, the missing parts that I'll keep to myself. There can be no cracks in the story. They'll say I should've reported it right away. They'll want to know why I waited. How can I answer without giving away my shame and showing my longing?

My fear is surely groundless. No one's paying attention to me. And if they are they probably think I'm just one more crazy tourist lost in Jerusalem. But even my friends were amazed to learn I was still here. "I thought you'd gone," Nurit said a week after I was supposed to fly home. I lied. I told her I had an open ticket and had decided at the last minute to stay a while longer.

I should've told them. This way, I can't find out what happened, so my dread just intensifies. But talking to Nurit or Eli I clam up after the first sentence.

"I met a young Armenian," I told Nurit.

"Where? In the Old City?" She looked skeptical. "Be careful."

"He's not like the men who hang out at the Jaffa Gate."

She eyed me with pity. "And how long did it take you to find that out?"

"About four days."

We laughed and moved on to something else.

Sometimes I imagine that it's all on tape—every humiliation, all our silly conversations, his awful friends, our lovemaking—every little part that I'm too ashamed to tell my friends. I can't bear to think of it. But when I do, when I picture the whole thing on-screen, I cringe, mortified. There's no excuse. Do what you want with that woman, I think. She's not worth defending.

One Friday afternoon, I met Anahita in the Old City. I'd decided to tell her. I thought I'd feel less embarrassed talking to her because she herself is Armenian. Anahita ran a bright little

tourist boutique in the Cardo, the ancient Roman arcade exca-
vated in the Jewish Quarter. The light in her shop was dazzling,
reflected in her mirrors and glass and gold and silver trinkets; it
made the street outside seem like a dark tunnel. A few steps away,
the Muslim Quarter languished in the lifeless hues of an inhospitable twilight, the stores dark and shuttered every afternoon in
protest. Only the rivulets of rainwater gave light, glistening as
they trickled through the cracks of paving stones. On the walls,
graffiti blossomed in riotous colors. My shame was written there,
glaring and obscene. "We fuck your women," it said, an insult to
humiliate the enemy. But the enemy no longer goes there, not
without a weapon. Even the tourists keep away, preferring to
spend their afternoons down at the Dead Sea.

I sat on a stool and watched Anahita sell a menorah. She
seemed bored by the transaction, naming the price in such a soft
voice that I couldn't hear what she said. Her smooth face gave
away nothing, not her thoughts nor her age. She always greeted
me with such indifference that I'd wonder whether she wanted
me there. Although she had volunteered her life story the first
time we met. She'd even told me about her parents and how
they'd survived persecution. She'd asked me to come again and
gave me the feeling that I'd found a friend.

Her customers, two wiry Frenchmen in gray tones from their
carefully trimmed hair down to their tasteful slacks, turned to go,
undecided and discouraged. Anahita took a half step toward them
and announced a new price. One pulled out his wallet in relief
and resignation.

"Tourists are dumb," she said, once the two were out of earshot.
"They'll buy anything from Jerusalem, even useless bits of rock."

I liked watching her there, standing among her glittering display cases in a sky-blue dress that made her skin look brighter and her eyes darker. Anahita was a bit plump, no longer young but still girlish, as if infinite possibilities still lay before her. She'd talked to me about most of the important things in her life, yet I still knew so little about her. When she was silent I couldn't begin to guess what she was thinking. And there was a lot of silence between her sentences; her words often seemed to drown in it. Actually, she knew nothing about the outside world that produced the tourists she despised. She had grown up in Abu Dis on the West Bank when it still belonged to Jordan, an only daughter, unmarried, a servant in her father's house. She had finally rebelled and moved to Jerusalem where a single woman can run a shop and live alone. Not entirely alone, though. She roomed in the Armenian convent.

At five o'clock she set the alarm system, locked the door, and pulled the iron gate closed, solemnly, as if every movement was a symbolic act of great significance. In the Jewish Quarter housewives were doing their last-minute shopping before the Sabbath, baguettes and pale-colored vegetables in their shopping bags.

Anahita led me past the convent doorkeeper and we walked through a labyrinth of corridors and up staircases onto the roof. The two whitewashed cubes jutting out of the flat rooftop were her rooms, each of which was covered with corrugated steel. Their iron doors were shedding chips of blue paint. My bedroom, she indicated, my kitchen. The evening wind caressed the rooftop cupolas. It grew cool as we sat at a table drinking Turkish coffee and eating grapes. Anahita faced the Old City wall behind which the sky had begun to light up in dark flames. I looked out at the Mosque of Omar. Its golden dome drew the waning red glare like a heavenly body illuminating the night.

"Do you think I can still fall in love at fifty-five?" she asked.

"Have you never been in love?" I said.

"Every so often a man would show some interest, but nothing would really come of it."

But her employer had big plans for her. "He trusts me," she said. "He lets me run the business any way I like. Maybe I'll even go to Europe one of these days." Then she looked young, like an overweight girl about to shake off a strict upbringing, eagerly anticipating her future.

"Things are going well for me now," she declared.

I felt close to her and wanted to promise that it was all possible, her own shop, trips to Europe, falling in love. I told her that she had good business sense and that it was never too late. And since we were talking about the future, she turned my cup over and read my fortune in the black coffee grounds, while the long howl of sirens announced the onset of the Sabbath.

"You should stick to West Jerusalem," she said, sounding just like all my Israeli friends. The coffee grounds gave her the occasion to drive the point home. "You see," she said, turning the black rim of the cup toward her, "there's danger lurking in the east, especially down in the valley, in Abu Tor and Silwan. And you shouldn't go to the Muslim Quarter, either."

"That's what everyone says," I protested.

"Visit the Israel Museum," she advised. I laughed. During my first week in Jerusalem I stayed in a kibbutz guesthouse, and every morning an old retiree kept asking me to go to the Israel Museum with him.

We looked out over the railing at the dark street below. Pious Jews and tourists rushed quietly toward the Western Wall. The sky was still holding onto a strip of faded red, but over the Old

City rooftops and the Mount of Olives it had cooled down to a clear, translucent green.

"I met a young Armenian," I said, and saw a wariness enter her eyes.

Did I imagine it? Was she suspicious right away, at the first mention of Sivan's name, or did it develop over time, little by little?

"Where did you meet him?"

"In the Jewish Quarter, at the Hurva Synagogue."

She said nothing.

"He said he was Catholic."

She shrugged her shoulders. Possible, but unlikely.

I couldn't read the expression on her smooth face, but the sense of closeness had vanished. Suddenly I felt heavy with loneliness and sorrow. Maybe it was the melancholy of a Friday night, or of the whole city, or maybe Anahita's sadness was contagious.

"Do you have the letter þ in your alphabet?" I asked, already knowing her answer.

"Why?"

"Because he can't pronounce it."

"Then he's Palestinian," she said. "We've even got two þ sounds. Palestinians often try to pass as Armenians, so be careful."

"It's too late for that. Would an Armenian drive to Ramallah at night?"

"No Armenian would dare be caught on the West Bank at night. He's lying to you."

I didn't ask any more questions and she wasn't interested in my story. In her eyes, I had just become another dumb, naive tourist.

"Stick to West Jerusalem where you belong. You don't

understand East Jerusalem, you're putting yourself in all kinds of danger."

We sat a while longer looking at the glassy dark sky. A slender sickle of moon hung over the Mount of Olives like a gently curved blade. In two weeks it would be full and a month would have passed since Sivan disappeared. Strangely, when Anahita killed my last hope that he might have been telling the truth, I began to reclaim the affection I'd transferred to her in his absence. She had just become another woman who'd been cheated of her life. We both felt it was time for me to leave.

"Don't go back through the Zion Gate," she warned me. "It's too isolated, something might happen, be careful."

We felt our way through the convent's dark maze of stairways, hallways, and courtyards, finally arriving at Jacob's Church. The gate was locked. "I lived in a convent for a while," Sivan had told me, "but you have to be in by ten o'clock, so I moved out." At least he was well-informed.

The street was deserted and for the first time I felt afraid of walking through the Old City alone.

In the beginning I wasn't at all afraid, not even in Silwan, or Abu Tor or the Kidron Valley, places everyone warned me about. But then things started to happen almost every day, especially at the Central Bus Station, "disturbances," they were called. Suddenly, the lines of people waiting for buses would be herded into a corner by a nervous young woman soldier, or the station would be closed off altogether. The word spread quickly, bomb scare, one of many. Traveling on buses, I could measure the force and size of rocks thrown at the windows by the smudge of splintering glass left behind. Once, I discovered a bullet hole just above my head.

I didn't read the newspapers and trusted the tour guides who, seeing their incomes shrinking, swore you could go anywhere in Jerusalem, no one would touch a tourist. But I'd met tourists whose rented cars had been set alight. I learned to listen for small things casually mentioned, to interpret the message in people's eyes, and I began to pick up the slight restlessness in a crowd before someone yelled bomb scare, everyone out. More than once, I'd seen uniformed police in vans with barred windows stop in the middle of Jaffa Road and herd young men into the back, slamming the doors shut. No one ever stopped to look, no one ever inquired. "They're suspects, probably Arabs, it's just a fact of life here, you get used to it," people explained. Like everyone else I asked no questions. When the bomb squad closed off a street to detonate a stray package or unclaimed shopping bag I'd simply take a detour, like everyone else. I hardly even winced at the sound of the blast. But still, I became uneasy, edgily alert, as if there were special dangers waiting for me personally.

I had known Sivan for less than a week when I suggested we go up to the Mount of Olives for a view of the city at night, by the light of the moon.

"But it's dangerous," he said.

"Are you afraid?" I asked.

Then he insisted on going, as if the trip had become a test of his courage. He wanted to prove that he wasn't a coward, but he stole down Mount Zion past the stone houses of Silwan as if he were making his way through enemy lines. He dragged me across the stony slope so impatiently that I started to protest. "Keep quiet," he whispered, "it's dangerous here." I didn't know whether we were playing a game or whether we were in real danger. Sivan only loosened his grip once we reached the cemetery in the floor of the valley, where the bony white graves of the prophets and the sinister shadows put the fear of ghosts in you. Then we ran up the Mount of Olives. The cypresses loomed so high and dense in the night sky that I couldn't see the path through the blackness and lost all sense of direction. As we climbed over the rubble of a stone wall, I was startled to see the city spread out below us, moonlit and shimmering.

We sat on a wide stone slab and looked at Jerusalem until I was sure I'd fixed the image in my mind forever—the Dome of the Rock and Al Aqsa, with their gold and silver globes, the black mass of squat stone houses stacked one above the other, the distant glitterings of light which flickered and then died away. The air was sharp and cold, but we still made love in the piercing night wind, naked on our stone slab as if laid out for sacrifice. First, we slid our hands beneath each other's clothing for warmth, then we sheltered our nakedness from the wind with our loving, tender bodies, feeling every touch on bare skin, every downy hair ruffling under searching fingers. We were unpracticed with each other that first time, but every seeking, probing attempt unlocked a new and wondrous intimacy.

Sivan broke the silence when we heard a noise. As we slid off the edge of our stone slab and hunched down in the darkness of a rock pile overgrown with thorny brush and weeds, I thought, this is probably a tomb, we just made love on the grave of a prophet.

I remember the cypresses on the way back and a plain, unremarkable mosque to the right of a sharp bend in the path, and that we ran hand in hand without saying a word to each other. It wasn't until we were back in the Old City that Sivan kissed me, hard, as if I'd just saved his life.

"You think you can go anywhere you want," Frieda said, when I told her I'd been in the Old City, in the Hinnom Valley, or on Mount Zion. I said nothing about my midnight trip to the Mount of Olives.

"Don't you understand that we're at war?" she said. "Why do you deliberately put yourself in so much danger?"

"Come on, Frieda, you're exaggerating," I said. "I've seen plenty of Jews over there."

"It's Channa," she corrected me. "It's been Channa for fifty years."

But she'd always been Frieda to me; whenever my grandmother spoke of her it was Frieda she talked about. My grandmother was related to Martha and so was Frieda on her father's side, but they'd also been close friends. Which brings me to the real reason that I came to Jerusalem—I was looking for Martha. I came here because of her.

Frieda-Channa has an open house every Sunday and Thursday. On those afternoons I would take the bus out past the hills of Kiryat Yovel, beyond the shabby apartment blocks built in the fifties, where the slopes covered with thistles and olive trees drop off sharply in the direction of her isolated village, Ein Kerem. Few tourists ever came out this far, but there were usually a few young mothers sitting in the shade of pine trees while their children slid through the giant maw of a plastic park monster, and in the late afternoon, from Frieda-Channa's kitchen window, you could see lovers searching for a secluded spot among the bushes.

At night, Frieda would take me to the bus stop and would never forget, even if the bus was coming around the bend, to point out a rough-hewn stone by the roadside, engraved with the names of four dead commuters and the date of their killing. Pointing her finger, she'd remind me to at least be careful, even if I couldn't bring myself to show some common sense and move into her guest room. "Four innocent people, totally unsuspecting, stabbed on a beautiful spring afternoon by an Arab fanatic. They were doing nothing, just waiting for a bus, and you go walking around East Jerusalem in that getup you're wearing."

"Why don't you move to Tel Aviv, where it's safer?" I asked her.

She gave me a horrified look. "I built this city," she said. "The difference with you is that you're reckless. We're careful. We live with the danger, but we never forget it."

There were more and more things she couldn't forget. The house in Vienna from which her parents were deported in 1941. Every single piece of furniture, every household item, the view from the kitchen, the courtyard of linden trees, the wild grape vines, and the flower beds. For Frieda, the details of Vienna in the 1930s grew sharper and more vivid with each passing year. Even I could see her home in Vienna and smell the fragrance of linden here in Ein Kerem. I too could summon up the picture of her parents leaving their house with two suitcases in the damp gray dawn of a cold March day. That's the last image Frieda has of them, or perhaps just the last image she'll allow herself to impose on her visitor. Then followed a long silence in which we both separately traced their journey to its end. "I've never forgiven myself for not getting them out," she told me. "I tried, but not hard enough. If we'd had any idea of what was going to happen, I'd have done anything, I'd have done the impossible."

"What about Martha?" I asked.

The last time Frieda had seen her was in Salzburg, shortly before she emigrated to Palestine. Martha had married an artist, a Viennese man who divorced her later, after 1938, just as Frieda had expected. When they met in Salzburg, they were no longer close; they hardly had anything to say to each other.

"I was a Zionist," Frieda said, "and she was blind, blind and crazy in love with that man. He was a real charmer, anyone could see. But he was only interested in himself and had to be the center of attention. After the Anschluss, after her eyes had been opened, Martha wrote to me here in Jerusalem, but her letter took a number of detours before finally reaching me. It was postmarked Prague, but for all I knew, she might no longer have been alive when I read it. She wrote about emigrating. Not to Palestine, God forbid, but to England, Holland, or Switzerland. Me, all I ever wanted was to come here and build my own country. Not Martha. If there's one thing for sure, it's that she never came to Israel."

I said nothing. I was convinced Martha was here, but I didn't want to open up my obsession to Frieda's scrutiny.

Frieda went back to Vienna once, thirty years after she'd left. The city she returned to was strange to her, foreign. It took her eight hours to get up the courage to look at the house. "You can't imagine what it's like," she said, "living for thirty years with those images tormenting me, then coming back to a different city." Frieda found the neighborhood easily enough, even the street, but she circled the house for eight hours, walking around the core of her pain. "I couldn't do it," she admitted. "I could see the house from the end of the street. It was still standing, with the same facade, but I couldn't walk up to it and go in." She spent two days in Vienna and then went to Frankfurt, where her husband was born, and stayed two weeks with friends.

"Forgiveness, reconciliation,—I've got no use for those words," she said. "They mean nothing to me."

I visited Frieda twice a week and spent hours sitting with the two pieces of furniture she brought from Vienna, her little art nouveau desk, and a chest of drawers with rococo marquetry. She plied me with fruits and candy like a long-lost granddaughter and told me about a Jerusalem that no longer exists: the Old City before the War of Independence in 1948, the Jewish Quarter where she starved during the siege, Rehavia, the refined German neighborhood where she lived for thirty years. Some stories she told again and again: about the old woman holding her last egg in her hand during the siege, being so careful not to break it; about the cooking stove she improvised from a window grille; how hungry they had been and how hard it was for her to watch her child suffer. Her eyes shone when she described the Old City in those days, the Ethiopian monks living above the Church of the Holy Sepulcher, the Via Dolorosa, and the Muslim Quarter, "but I don't ever want to catch you going there," she would add. "One day, when there's peace, we'll go down there together and I'll show you everything. You haven't even begun to scratch the surface of Jerusalem. There's always more, it's inexhaustible—the views, the little hidden courtyards with their ancient trees and fountains, you have to know where they are otherwise you can walk right past them."

I didn't tell her that I'd seen more than she knew. Still, she was right, I hadn't discovered her Jerusalem.

"One day they'll slaughter us all," she said calmly as she put fruit and sandwiches on the table. She could have been talking about the siesta she always took between two and four, her voice was so impassive. "Not yet, though," she went on. "We have the best army in the region, but it's inevitable."

I didn't tell Frieda that my plane ticket was no longer valid, and she had no idea about what kind of life I'd been living. I kept wanting to tell her, sure that she'd understand. But then she'd start giving me her advice—"Don't go to the souk on Fridays when they're all wound up after the sermon at Al Aqsa Mosque, and if you can't manage to keep away from there, wear a longer skirt"—and she'd show me that rough memorial by the bus stop and I would feel as if I was the assassin, I the traitor.

Sivan and I almost never talked about politics. Just once at the very beginning and then never again, at least not until the night in Ramallah. I could have tried to draw him out, but he'd put the subject off-limits after our first conversation and besides, I'd had enough of the same old worn-out discussions. I'd heard all the arguments on both sides and, in any case, if you knew who you were talking to, you could guess what they had to say. Arab or Jew? That was the all-important question in Jerusalem, and without an answer there was no conversation and no trust. For the most part, Jerusalemites don't have to ask, they can tell at first sight. If necessary, there are indirect ways to put the question, too. "Where are you from?" "Where do you live?" and "Do you have family in Israel?" are all ways to extract the information without going straight to the heart of the matter. But if you have to ask, then you can also be deceived.

I was standing in the ruins of the Hurva Synagogue looking

at a perfect arch—a flawless half circle of stone, stretching tall up to the heavens, towering above the entire Jewish Quarter, yet leading nowhere. It was a triumphal arch of futility. I was craning my head back in amazement, thinking about its lack of function and how that might enhance its beauty. A tour group was just leaving the ruin when a young man came over and asked if he could tell me more about Hurva. I thought he lived there and was not proud of his neighborhood so I said, yes, of course, why not? Then he led me to a plaque put up by the tourist bureau on which the history of the synagogue was written in two languages.

"I can read too," I said, amused.

"Where are you from?" he asked.

"New York."

"But you don't have an American accent."

"I grew up in Austria."

"Are you Jewish?"

"Yes, and you?"

"Armenian."

Much later he said, "Do you know what I thought the first time I saw you?" And then he hesitated, as if he'd been about to say something outrageous. "You'll be insulted."

"Maybe, but now I want to know."

"I thought you were an Arab, you were so beautiful."

I wasn't insulted, but I didn't make anything of it, either.

"Where do you live?" I asked.

"In the Jewish Quarter."

I believed that, too, without giving it a second thought. He might have been testing me, trying to establish the limits of my knowledge. As if, in a city so strictly segregated by religion and nationality, an Armenian would live in the Jewish Quarter. But I swallowed it.

In my defense, I knew few Armenians and had never considered where they might live. This man seemed pleasant and friendly and when he offered to show me around the city, I saw no reason to turn him down.

And I was attracted to him. I watched him out of the corner of my eye, taking note of his easy walk and his athletic physique, slender and willowy. He looked as if he were still growing, with his oval, childlike face and large black eyes.

"How long are you staying?" he asked, as we were standing in front of the Burnt House. Again, he had nothing special to tell me about the place, and there was no plaque outside. I suppose he thought I had some particular interest in ancient buildings.

"Five more days and then I'm going to Tiberias."

"Can I come with you?"

I laughed. "How old are you?"

"Twenty-four. And you?"

"Old enough to be your mother."

"That doesn't matter. I like older women."

I switched to politics because I was curious. "What's the Armenian position in the Arab-Israeli conflict?" I asked.

He held out his slender hands like the trays on a scale. "Here are the Jews, and here are the Arabs. The Armenians are stuck between them, we can't afford to spoil things with either side."

That made sense. I recalled the shuttered quiet of the Armenian Quarter, the reticence of the Armenian merchants in the souk.

We sat in a recess in the Old City wall and looked beyond the white, one-story houses of Silwan into the Judean Desert, bathed in the peach tones of the late afternoon light. On the horizon the Dead Sea quivered in the haze like a fata morgana.

"What would you do with this country?" I asked him. "I don't live here, so I can't really come down on one side or another."

During my stay, I'd asked everyone this question, Jews and Arabs, and had received elaborate answers that spun such a web of allegories and parables that both question and response were obscured in the luxuriant flourish of poetry. I'd also heard raving, hateful responses that had frightened me and simple, straight-forward ones, rooted in reason, which I then repeated for the benefit of my Jewish friend, Eli, who claimed you couldn't talk to "them," the other side.

"You're naive," he said to me. "You mistake simplicity for truth. Anyway, you'll never get an honest answer to a question like that."

Sivan's response was reasonable and clear, and seemed sincere. "But I don't see a problem," he said. "Two states, side by side, the details to be negotiated, and Jerusalem an international zone under UN protection."

Maybe that should have tipped me off. Probably his stories about visiting Iraq, Egypt, and Syria with his father should have made me wary. And then there were his nasty jokes about Israelis. My ear is very sensitive to anti-Semitic nuances; I pick them up easily. Yet I never felt insulted by Sivan, and I don't now, looking at our relationship in the cold light of reason. I have nothing to be ashamed of.

They could all be spies and terrorists, collaborators working for one side or the other or both at the same time. There's no end of possibilities and everyone else is better informed than I. But now I'm involved too. I can't walk around Jerusalem without feeling mired in a swamp of ambiguities which I'll never understand. Anahita could be a spy. She knows everyone and always predicts what's going to happen next, then explains away her foresight with her coffee grounds.

Like the gingerhaired shopkeeper. Anahita told me all about his shady deals and his trouble with the police. He seemed to know me, too. He summed me up right away, as soon as I entered the Old City through the Jaffa Gate. He saw that I was intimidated by the way people stared, grabbing at me with their eyes the moment I stepped into the souk. He knew I would take a blind turn down a dead end street and end up outside his shop. All he had to do was call out softly and I, curious, turned around like a sleepwalker and followed him into his shop. He asked about my earrings and identified them as Bohemian garnet, not precious but a family heirloom. Why did he choose those earrings, of all things to catch my attention? He astounded me. What else did he know? He prepared a pot of Turkish coffee, as if this were some conspiratorial tryst. God knows what he put in it while I was stealing glances at the shop. Semiprecious stones rolled around loose in cardboard boxes, Oriental garnet, Eilat stone, and hematite. The walls were draped with sayings from the Koran. He's religious, I thought, maybe Hamas. Evil intentions thickened the air like a mysterious odor while I listened uncomfortably to the compliments he proffered. He spoke in German without first asking where I came from and his accent was slight.

"Didn't I see you in the American Colony Hotel?" he asked, referring to the East Jerusalem hub of foreign journalists and peace activists. "Are you politically involved?" He was probing my alliances, I thought, checking whether I was a Jewish leftist and therefore trusting and malleable, ready to betray my own side.

"I haven't been there recently," I answered, evasively.

"Maybe a few weeks ago?"

"Possibly."

"I've been watching you," he said. "You're independent and ready to take risks, but you're ignorant and dangerous." I was fascinated and willed him to continue.

"At first you were bored, and now you're frightened. That's good. You're looking for someone who understands you, and that's me. I know more than you think. I know you." He pressed a garnet necklace on me.

"I don't want it," I said. I looked at his red hair and the freckles on his face and hands flowing into one another like a sunburn. He was at once repulsive and irresistible; I should've left then but it was impossible to get up and go. I hungered for his words, what he still had to say about me, what he knew of Sivan. I felt he was conveying a cryptic message for me to decode. I sat in his boutique entranced. I couldn't get enough; he was pure poison. I didn't dare look at my watch, fearing I might break the spell. The air in the tiny closed room was suffocating, full of erotic vibrations.

"And you? Do you often go to the American Colony Hotel?" I asked, to take back control.

He brushed aside my question with the flick of his wrist as if it were a bothersome fly. "Look," he said, "things are very different from what you think. There's no truth in politics, in negotiations. It's all talk and more talk. I can help you find what's been missing in your life. No one chooses to stay in the dark if they have a choice, and you always have a choice."

"I have to go," I pleaded.

"You're not in that much of a hurry," he said. "You've gotten yourself into something you don't understand. You don't even know which questions to ask, and you wouldn't know what to do with the answers anyway. Go to the café on Nablus Street, they might be able to help you. Don't tell anyone who sent you, I'll wait for you here. Way up Nablus Street, almost to the end, on the right."

He pressed the necklace on me again, holding it up to the light. "Pure fire, it suits you, not the Eilat stone, it's too cold. One hundred shekels."

"I don't wear necklaces, I don't want it."

"You drank my coffee," he said. "All the time you've been sitting here I haven't been able to sell a thing."

I took it for eighty shekels, I don't know why. It lies in the cool depths of my shoulder bag, and when I touch it I can feel the man's threatening pull throughout my body, up to the hair on my neck. "You'll be back," he said at the door. "I know you'll be back."

I fell into the street in the stagnant heat of an early afternoon, breathing hard, as if I'd just escaped a brutal embrace. I left the Old City through the gate I'd entered and sat, nursing my fear and confusion, under the crooked pines beneath the city wall. I was nervous and miserable, vexed by a nameless desire, not for the shopkeeper, not even for Sivan. I spent the rest of the afternoon on the crumbling steps of a secluded stairway high above the red roofs of a city in which I no longer felt safe, trying to form a clear thought.

A young boy came down the steps and fixed me in a provocative, insolent stare. Everyone knows, I thought, even him. Why else would he be looking at me like that? I clung to my broken step as if to a leaky ship; the pines and cedars whispered across the slope and rubbed their dry branches together; the dull, chalky white of rain-washed stones glimmered through the foliage. It would be easy, I thought, to drop through the cracks in the stone into some hideous, unseen underworld.

In this state, I showed up at Anahita's shop shortly before closing time. Shadows darkened the narrow streets as Hasidim hurried to evening prayer at the Western Wall, their footsteps soft and swift.

"Look at this," I said, showing her the necklace. "I paid eighty shekels. Did I get taken?"

Anahita weighed the stones in her hand, held them up to the light, and looked at them for a long time under her magnifying glass. "They're real all right, just badly strung. Where did you get them?"

"A shop near the Jaffa Gate."

"A man with red hair, lots of freckles?"

"Yes, do you know him?"

"Sure, Ihab from Hebron. A swindler, but very smart. People from Hebron are supposedly descended from the Crusaders, that's why they're so fair-skinned. Be careful," she warned, "they say he's a collaborator, he's supposed to be working with the Shin Bet, but no one has been able to prove anything. In fact, every few weeks they pick him up and take him to the police station, but he's always out in a couple of hours, and his business is flourishing."

I stared at her white, fine-boned hands warming the garnet necklace and wondered again how she knew so much.

I stay on. Each time I come I stay longer than the last. On my first trip it was Martha, then it was Gilbert and the kibbutz, now it's Sivan, who's been swallowed up without a trace. Frieda, Eli, and

Nurit keep asking me what I'm looking for, then offer advice on how to become an immigrant.

Every ten years or so I give in and decide to make my stay permanent. I plan a quick trip back to Europe to pick up my things, but then it's ten years later, and I return with a different passport and a new traveling companion. When I'm in Jerusalem I long to be embraced, like a returning lover, to be invited behind the stone walls and the cypresses into the sweet, hidden life of the city.

Twenty years ago the signs of war were still visible. The valley dividing East and West Jerusalem was strewn with rolls of barbed wire, empty shells, and nettles. Twenty years ago I met Gilbert on the Via Dolorosa. He was wearing an embroidered shirt from the souk and his long, dark hair fell almost to his belt. The last rains had dried in the earth weeks before and bougainvillea blossoms cascaded over the roofs and ledges. I was trying to locate Frieda Lipkin, to whom Martha, my grandmother's cousin, had sent a letter shortly before she disappeared in 1940. It was a ridiculous undertaking since Frieda might well have changed her name, and I was too young and shy to ask the authorities for help in tracking her down.

Most of the time I wandered around the Old City, dazzled by the bazaars, their smells and brilliant colors, and sustained by the vague hope that I was on the trail of some important secret— at any moment something dramatic could happen. Every gesture, every greeting, every smile seemed to me like a covert sign, a code I had to crack. Things grew dense with the burden of meaning I imagined they contained. Everything reminded me of something else, and nothing was what it seemed to be.

A horse came trotting down the Via Dolorosa, carrying a

Crusader, a Roman legionnaire, or a Saracen. His appearance was surely significant and I wanted a picture. A young boy blocked my view, but instead of leaving my field of vision, as I tried to coax him to do, he knocked the camera out of my hands and was about to deliver another blow.

"Are you all right?" A tall Frenchman with long hair pulled me away from the spot. I don't remember how I felt, only a conviction cherished for twenty years that nothing will ever compare with that first love. Without a word, we walked to the Western Wall hand in hand. It was simply the right thing to do. Never again did I have that certainty of having cracked the code and revealed the secret. I had no doubts.

I've never been able to retrace the path we took to the wall. The war rubble has been cleared and the landscape changed, but I don't believe that's why I couldn't find our route. I couldn't even find the nook in the wall where I began to cry, embarrassed by my lack of experience. As I fled from Gilbert in shame, he yelled at me to meet him the next day at the windmill.

That night, I lay awake wondering what my older, more experienced friend would say. Incredibly stupid and reckless is what she called me in the morning. "You don't know a thing about him. You don't even speak the same language," she said. I went to the windmill anyway and, leaving my friend in the youth hostel, I moved into his kibbutz near Ashkelon, on the Mediterranean coast.

The rest of my life pales when I hold it up to that time with Gilbert. The city of the Philistines nestled among eucalyptus roots, the sharp shadows of palm trees, white, powdery sand, and a pale, calm sea. In the dark blue Ashkelon sky, the stars appeared as large and bright as they had in the pictures of my childhood, joined by glittering threads of light. The hot sandy path winding between the kibbutz huts; the fragrance of the mint we suspended in boiling water to make tea; the timeless rhythm of the summer heat, its waxing and waning—all these marked a present untroubled by the future. Once I told a kibbutznik that we had found paradise; he laughed and said I was either in love or just plain crazy.

Gilbert and I shared a room that was just large enough for the two mattresses we had pushed together, a chair, a table, a narrow locker, and our Shiva and Buddha hanging on the walls. Just above the mattresses at eye level a volunteer had scrawled the words to "Lay Lady Lay." We must have fought, too. Once I came back from Tel Aviv with a plane ticket and packed my rucksack. But I stayed, got up next morning and the morning after that, at four thirty, as always, and took my place on the tractor in my heavy boots and big blue shorts. Still drowsy, we'd ride out to the fruit orchards. The trunks of the pear trees would still be damp from the sprinklers. Snakes would crawl into the shade of the thistles growing at the base of the cypresses. Sometimes there'd be one as thick as an arm lying dead in the road. We'd talk very little while we picked. The day would grow hot. We'd sit at the edge of the plantation and drink weak, hot coffee, burning our fingers on the plastic cups.

There must have been some tension in this idyll. In the room next door there were scenes between David, the Moroccan classical music lover, and Sharon, who filled their nights with pop music in order to show her disdain for everything traditional. In the middle of all this, Gilbert played his guitar for hours every day.

"It's a madhouse," said Shmulik, a kibbutznik who lived in one of the stone houses next to our clubhouse. "What are you doing with that spaced out French guy? You're much too sane and mature for him. Don't you want to move in with me?"

I had no intention of ever leaving Gilbert or the kibbutz. I had found my family, I thought. Here was my destiny and the man of my life. I loved his earnestness and his passion as we talked about his ideas late into the night. Dancing, loving, playing, he did everything in excess. He was a seeker, he said, a wandering philosopher who regularly came to blows over ideas. But he could also be very gentle, almost motherly in his concern. He'd listen to me and I was certain he understood as I did the darkness and shame that lay over my childhood.

On Friday afternoons we'd sweep the sand from our cabin and decorate our table with a rose stolen from the greenhouse. We'd imagine our future: one day we'd speak Hebrew together, have children, and live in one of the stone kibbutz houses. I'd expected to search for years to find my adult life, but it had come upon me suddenly, after I'd barely escaped the confines of home. Kibbutz life was seamless, providing a net you couldn't fall out of, from the cucumbers and tomatoes always cut precisely the same way for breakfast, to the candles and freshly ironed shirts on Friday evening, and the Sabbath mornings under the pale shade of the eucalyptus trees on the beach, where the heat melted away the last traces of decadent, bourgeois concepts like time and reason.

I know that I was happy, and in my happiness dumb and blind. Ashkelon is not in paradise but half an hour from Gaza, an hour from Hebron. I was shielded by a shimmering veil of sun and pleasure, I was untouched by any language I really knew. I hope everyone there has long forgotten the euphoric volunteer.

Twenty years later, I was replaying the experience, shifting in and out of double realities, mixing up layers of memory in much the same way that the ancient stones of Jerusalem were used over and over in the city's many resurrections, making a mess of history.

When I met Gilbert, Yemin Moshe was a nineteenth-century slum. Now it's a jewel, the tiny stone houses, restored to their original beauty, rise above a stunning view of the Old City, and the windmill is a popular meeting point for tourists. Spotlights go up for the music festival at the Sultan's Pool, and a summer crafts fair brings out artisans selling painted velvet cushions and dangling Yemenite-style silver earrings. We spent a lot of time down there, Sivan and I, under an olive tree with a crooked trunk, surrounded by burnt tufts of grass and cigarette stubs. Leaning on our elbows, we'd look at each other, we never tired of looking at each other.

"You have beautiful eyes," I said.

"Are you happy?" he asked, the tips of his fingers tracing my lips, my eyebrows, my chin. He took my face in both hands. Even when he was so very close his eyes were open. "Do you like this?" he asked with his eyes, with his gentle hands, hands I trusted. These hands would never hurt me, I thought. His body was so familiar to me it could have been shaped from my dreams. The Hinnom Valley below lay parched and deserted in the summer heat. Now and then a passerby would briefly look our way, but I had no interest in anything other than the man right next to me. We came here in the evenings, too, to watch the drift of day into night among the yellow agaves, brilliant acacias, and young cypresses. It almost became a ritual.

Now the moon is a narrow shaving, a white feather sailing

above the desert ravines. I still come here in the evenings, partly to torment myself, but also hoping Sivan can't resist the memory any more than I can. I freeze as soon as the wind comes up.

"What do you feel for me?" Sivan had asked, his eyes full of urgency, even desperation. I evaded the question. If I didn't say it, then it couldn't be true, I thought. If I didn't think it, then it didn't exist. Words change feelings, words shake things up. Unspoken, they remain suspended and can't be distorted.

"I like you," I said affectionately. He was obviously disappointed with my answer. "And you?" I asked.

He was always saying, "I feel." He called me a rationalist. Since our first afternoon in the Jewish Quarter we spoke English; he had no patience with my Hebrew, it seemed to annoy him. And he refused to get drawn into quarrels—he'd clam up, leaving me stranded with all my arguments. Sometimes I sensed in him a bitter reserve that barely masked his clenched brutality.

"I can't tell you, you wouldn't believe me," he replied. Now he looked like a defiant child refusing to give anyone the satisfaction of seeing him confess to anything.

"I love you," I said, and was terrified.

"With your head, or your feelings?"

"My feelings, my body,"

"I love you, too," he said.

A moment's light-headedness and it was over, gone. But whoever he really was—a liar, a playboy, a terrorist—he spoke the truth. His body quivered in the silence that followed. It seemed that I could see all the way through Sivan's eyes into his head. Now I look back at that afternoon like a landscape under water—warped, uncertain. When I doubt him, when I feel betrayed or overcome with shame and anger, a wave of hate washes through me and I want revenge.

Sivan stared at Mount Zion with a remote look. He seemed like someone listening for an inaudible sound, always on the alert and poised to take flight.

"What are you thinking about?" I asked.

"I have an idea," he said. "I don't like living here, I haven't for a long time. What's it like in New York? Can I come back with you?"

I didn't have to think for very long. There was no place for him, for all kinds of reasons. There were laws, a person couldn't just move to New York. And my life was rational, while this love was not.

"It's impossible." I shook my head. "What would you do there?"

"I'm an interpreter. I speak four languages fluently."

"You wouldn't be happy, you'd be homesick. I'm a foreigner there too, everything's different. Eventually, in a year, six months, I'm going to go back to Europe."

"I've been away before," he protested, with hurt in his voice. "I can adjust."

I shook my head again.

"We love each other," he pleaded.

"It won't be enough. It'll be too hard."

Sivan fell silent. Evening had just begun. The tables in front of the restaurants and bars were occupied, the doors of boutiques were open, and the Russian street musicians were playing their set pieces. We parted between the Arab cemetery and

Independence Park. Numb, I glided between the pedestrians, not ready to let the experience slip out of the present into memory. With my eyes half closed, I will it to stay.

The wheelchair cripple with the angelic face, stationed at his regular spot, called out to me. "Hey, honey, going home already?" Once I was back in my hotel room, I lay down on the bed and let joy course through my body.

Whenever Sivan met me in West Jerusalem he seemed nervous. At first, I thought he just didn't want to be seen with me. He'd wait at the same street corner on a concrete bollard, his hands resting between his knees, leaning slightly forward, his face screwed up with tension. He was always there before me and seemed relieved when I came around the corner, but he never moved close to me. He'd walk at a distance like a casual acquaintance, not touching me, hardly even looking in my direction. Only when we reached the isolated bushes marking the East-West seam would Sivan put his arms around me and become animated.

"Pick me up at my hotel," I suggested at first. I felt there was nothing to hide and no reason to be furtive.

"I don't want to make problems for you," he said. Even late at night he wouldn't bring me all the way to the hotel door.

"Is it because you're Armenian?" I asked.

Nurit warned me. "No one likes to see Jewish women with Arab men, things could get unpleasant."

"But he's an Armenian," I protested.

"It's basically the same thing, and besides, he's Christian."

I wouldn't believe her. I didn't want to feel like an outsider just because I was with the wrong man. Still, I found myself hoping that none of my friends would see us together, and I convinced myself that I was simply respecting his privacy. It never occurred to me that his uneasiness, which later blossomed into scarcely controlled panic, might have another cause. I was irritated that we didn't stroll hand in hand through the pedestrian mall and never sat together at a cafe. Whenever I spent an evening with Eli or Nurit, I'd think about Sivan with regret, longing to respond to him spontaneously and meet in places where I felt secure and comfortable.

Instead, we'd steal through the parks like criminals, crouch under the cover of bushes, make love beneath scrawny olive trees in Hinnom Valley and the Muslim cemetery. Fleeing from noises, listening for footsteps, we were suspended in a no-man's land between East and West Jerusalem always in sight of the Old City wall. We'd hear Israeli folk music piped out of hotel lobbies while stray cats skulked around our hiding place. We'd lie deep in the shadows, concealed even from the moon, happy, yes, but cast out and banished. After making love we had no blanket to crawl under so we'd pull our clothes over our naked bodies and lie for a while in the dampness until the cold drove us out. Dazed, we'd walk back to the bright, lively streets as if we had traveled from a distant world and were having trouble rejoining this one.

Once we were back in the crowd, Sivan would check over his shoulder, swiftly, back and forth in all directions, while pushing quickly through the crowd. I gave up trying to make him feel at ease in West Jerusalem, this shy native of Mount Zion. Not that he looked any different from the other men on the street, tall, dark, and slender as he was, with the same light step and short black curls down to the nape of his neck. Every day he wore a freshly ironed shirt, spotless jeans, white socks, and running shoes, as neat and well-groomed as a model student from a good family. Women looked at him; no one else. I would have noticed.

But his insecurity was contagious. I found myself searching strangers' faces warily to see what they might be thinking of us as we made our way through Jerusalem's rush hour to our regular secluded spot, where we'd watch the city wall in the changing evening light.

"It doesn't matter where I go," Sivan said early on, "I'll always come back here."

"To Jerusalem?" I asked.

He shook his head and pointed up to the slope overgrown with low yellow brush and scruffy, windswept pines.

"The Zion Gate," he said ceremoniously, as if he were uttering an oath or a threat. I had the feeling his declaration was aimed at me but it made no sense. Why should he need to stake a claim to the Zion Gate?

"No one's going to take it away from you," I said.

He lit a cigarette and glared intently through the smoke which he exhaled in short bursts. Hostility shrouded him like a cold layer of air. His arm circled my waist, but he was still alone and far away.

$\mathcal{O}$ne Saturday afternoon, several weeks ago, I met Nurit in a hotel lobby. She was chain-smoking, decked out like a Persian queen in black silk, with luxuriant long, dark hair and large kohl-rimmed eyes. Somehow we skipped the usual polite questions and jumped straight into a conversation about politics, which lasted the entire afternoon. I learned that she was a sharp, rebellious woman who loathed illusions but loved dreams in her own paradoxical way. After that first afternoon, not a day went by when we didn't see each other.

She showed me the hidden Jerusalem, the enchanted alcoves and fabulous gardens behind the nondescript walls, places I would never find on my own. And whenever I'd break out in an enthusiastic cry of delight she'd tell me, with an ironic grin, "You know, all of this has its price." She loved Jerusalem, but insisted it was an impossible place to live in, moody and difficult.

"You should settle down here," she said. "There's nowhere else with so much beauty and spirituality. It'll ruin you, though, in the end you'll be a wreck, a bundle of nerves, ready for the madhouse."

Nurit passed the days at the window of her small bookstore with a cigarette in her hand. She seemed to know the news long before it was broadcast on the radio. Her easy but thoughtful manner attracted all kinds of people burning to discuss matters of the soul and unburden their passions and opinions. Occasionally, mid-sentence, she'd look probingly into my eyes, as if searching out a secret I might be withholding, and I wondered whether my subterfuge had begun to show.

Every time we parted I thought, next time I'll tell her, she will understand, she trusts me. But sitting in the garden of some coffeehouse or other talking about religious extremism in Jerusalem or Israeli claustrophobia, my small confessions seemed petty, negligible.

Nurit urged me to adopt an "Eastern" way of thinking, and there were times I thought I was on the way to doing just that. "There's never one single truth," she said. "There are many and they all coexist. Our mentality is Oriental, we don't deal in ideas, but in stories and allegory, we speak poetry and can live with a balance of opposites. You, you're always talking about justice, but really you're just self-righteous."

"Who's 'we'?"

"The Orientals, the Sephardic Jews and the Arabs. I don't feel Jewish," she once said, pausing to enjoy the shock effect of what she'd just said. "I feel Eastern and so I understand the Arabs better than I understand the Europeans."

She was trying to provoke me and she managed it. I thought of my German cousins who always looked good in dirndl skirts. I was better than them, different from them. Later, in school, I clung to my sense of superiority; it was my secret. It protected me from almost every kind of humiliation. When Nurit told me about the setbacks she suffered as the immigrant child of Iranian parents, I knew what she was talking about, though her story wasn't the same as mine. I didn't let on about me but was drawn back to her bookshop every day, if only for a cup of coffee. She gave me Hebrew children's books, good for beginning readers. I brought them back whenever I was done, but I got stuck on *Winnie the Pooh*, a book which contained great wisdom, according to Nurit, Oriental wisdom.

"Where are you headed?" she asked, as I got up to leave.

"The Old City."

"Then be back here before it gets dark."

"I thought you had such great affection for Orientals?"

"Just because I understand them doesn't mean I'm blind. Wariness is a survival strategy and anyway, there is no solution for our problem with our neighbors, don't let anyone try to tell you there is."

"They're not the only people in East Jerusalem," I protested.

"My friend Eli lives there. You should meet him. You don't have to make a date with Eli—you just run into him. He's always in a hurry but still has time to talk."

I had met Eli by chance eight years ago. He was a medical student and shared a room with a Hasidic calligrapher in a deserted part of the Jewish Quarter. Now he lived in East Jerusalem, and other things about him were new too, like his fez and the embroidered, ankle-length kaftan he'd begun wearing. I couldn't tell whether he had on a pair of pants beneath it. Nobody took any notice of him there, as if it were natural for a man to want to look like his grandfather in the mellah of Marrakesh. He'd had several wives at once, and Eli was working on that, too. He liked to say it was his national duty given the number of surplus women after so many wars. Still, for all his talk he lived with his wife and children and limited his activities to massage and homeopathic remedies. Would I like him to demonstrate?

"What happened to your medical studies?" I asked him.

"I finished years ago, but I prefer to heal people with natural treatments and the powers of the Kabbala."

"And living in East Jerusalem is your contribution to Arab-Israeli dialogue?"

"What are you talking about?" he said. "Arab-Israeli dialogue? There's no way for us to trust each other. But I have friends here—I grew up with Arabs, you know."

Eli is one of my best friends. I rarely see him, only once every four or five years, but we immediately find our way back to each other. Even so, I couldn't picture the milestones in his life, not his childhood in Morocco nor his youth in Israel in the sixties. In fact, we didn't agree on much—I didn't understand his culture and had no intention of trying to enlighten him about mine. The one thing we shared was our religion, and we didn't see eye to eye on that either.

With Sivan I would suddenly and inexplicably think about Eli. Not that I'd ever been in love with Eli, but it was his openness that I missed in Sivan. He'd explain the Kabbala to me on an overcrowded bus waving both his hands and talking so loudly that other passengers would start to chime in and point out his errors. He possessed the whole city and everything in it, the tourists, the Muslims, the Christians. He'd show me the great sites, touching the buildings with pride: "Look at this, ten meters long, just imagine what it was like to carry these colossal blocks!" Every stone in the city wall, every tower, everything belonged to him and he'd offer it all with great generosity, "Come, live here, you love Jerusalem, you should stay, it's your country, all Jews should live here."

When he'd leave me to deal with something I'd know why he was going and when he'd be back. With Sivan, I had no idea, not where he went, nor where he lived, nor what he ate—despite our closeness he was a stranger to me, and only became more so as time went on. In fact, he was the most perfect stranger I'd ever known, which might explain my obsession. I never did succeed in penetrating his secrets. It's possible he invented everything he told me; the one sure thing with him was what he hadn't said, that and my suspicions, the thoughts I willed away along with my creeping apprehension. He was unhappy in Jerusalem, trapped in a narrow world demarcated by the Old City and the Mamilla Cemetery. He was always running from something; any inclination he had to clown around was quickly defeated by his air of loneliness and depression. He loved me and suffered because of it—possibly he believed I could liberate him. At the same time, he cold-bloodedly used me. On whose orders?

His memories, his images, the sounds and smells that were the stuff of his world, all the things that had gone into making Sivan lie beyond the limits of my imagination, I cannot know them and my dreams cannot summon them. And it is this—his history and his essence—that disturbs me, torments me even, because it divided us from the beginning. My failure toward him was a failure of empathy and fantasy. I could see the Jerusalem of his childhood and imagine growing up in the shadow of the Old City, its walls chalky white in the morning and unearthly in their evening glow. I knew his landscape, the olive trees nestling in the shade of the wall and the cobblestones, smooth like river pebbles. But I will never see Jerusalem with a child's eyes—it will never be the only world I know, as it is for a child. I've never even been inside a Muslim or Armenian home. With which words did he name the world that opened up to him? What did he call the tastes, the colors, the moments that shaped his mind? How can I say that I loved him? But I did. It is the one certainty I still have.

11

Jerusalem is like a village in spite of the size of its population or the city's rapid spread over the hills in the west and the desert in the east. Despite its hustle and frenzy, Jerusalem still feels static, as if the whole city is stalled in place, waiting. I see the same faces over and over again, even I, a foreigner. Then there are the Jerusalem fixtures, professional idlers stationed at the same spot during the same shift, as if watching people was their sole occupation. A cluster of restless teenagers outside the Damascus Gate, men hawking postcards by the Old City wall—they all seem to be on guard, suspended in a state of expectation, their peddling a front for some other activity.

Of course, the tourists have no inkling of this other Jerusalem. They scurry about, full of energy and enthusiasm, falling into every conceivable trap. The locals pluck their strings, picking out tunes at will. Even the children are virtuosi, with a few beguiling words at the ready, something for everyone, a greeting in every language. They can read you from your hair and skin color, from the way you walk and stop and look, whether you're traveling alone and looking for adventure, whether you know where you're going or are ripe for a diversion. With a fortune-teller's intuition, at once precise and elusive, the locals can produce exactly the right sentence to pique your curiosity, pulling you in with suggestive compliments, seductive promises, and luxurious bouquets of words. "They think they're superior, better than everyone else, the Americans and Europeans," Nurit said. "They talk down to us as if we're children but they know nothing about us and they never will. We're the ones who've got their number."

Anahita said the same thing. "Look, we sell to their weaknesses, it's our livelihood."

At heart, they despise foreigners and usually have a derogatory phrase or sentence for each group.

"Germans," Sivan once said, as we approached a loud group of girls.

"How can you tell?"

"Only Germans make that silly laugh."

I heard a shriek and sure enough, once we were close to them, I heard them speaking German.

And what did he call me, which phrase did he use, the first time he saw me at the Hurva Synagogue? Not-so-young single woman looking for excitement? Sivan—a pimp with a mission, a honey trap for a woman traveling alone on a good passport—saw right away that I'd be an easy mark as long as he could satisfy my yearning for a romantic return to my youth.

"Why me?" I asked at the beginning.

"Because you're beautiful."

I can't let myself think that he might have been using me; it hurts too much. At the same time, I can't just close my eyes and plead innocence, it's too late for that. When I dwell on it for long enough, I just want to go straight to the police and tell them everything.

Sometimes I think that the thin flow of traffic between East and West Jerusalem would come to a complete halt were it not for trusting foreigners like me. The city would simply seize up, petrify, like the beggar who camps out at the pedestrian mall in Zion Square. He's there all hours of the day, even in the scorching midday heat, swathed in rags from head to toe, layer upon filthy layer, coat and muffler, a scarf around his head and a cap on top of that. He sits inert like a stuffed animal, as if he hasn't moved a muscle in years. He must know everything and have seen everything; actually, he's probably spying for someone, too.

Jerusalem is like a village. Even I have a few casual acquaintances who call out my name when they see me, some of whom I go out of my way to avoid. Adam, for example, but he changes his turf, so I don't always manage to avoid him.

We first met when he sat down next to me in the shade and offered me a cigarette. There's very little shade at midday, so he moved close to me.

"What's your name?" I asked him.

"Adam," he said. "My mother's from Italy, that's why I like European women."

"What do you do when you're not hanging out here?"

"I repair cars, but really I'm studying at the Technion in Haifa."

But he didn't know much about Haifa and quickly turned to

women. He loved them all and had lots of girlfriends, American, Dutch, German. "Maybe I'll emigrate," he said. "I don't really like it here. How about a disco tonight?" he went on.

"It's Friday night. Where are you going to find a disco?"

He bit his lower lip. "We'll go before it gets dark."

"How stupid do you think I am?" I asked. "Why don't you find yourself an Israeli girl?"

"They don't trust me."

"I don't trust you either."

"Will I see you tomorrow?"

"No, I'm going to Jericho," I lied.

"Take me with you?"

"The West Bank is dangerous," I said, looking him in the eye. "Aren't you afraid?"

Instead of answering he shouted, "I love you!"

Sometimes I see him by the youth hostel in Nahalat Shiva, in West Jerusalem, the absolute outer limit of his territory.

"How do you know he's lying?" I asked Nurit.

"Easy. He says his name's Adam or Avi but it's really Ali. But you don't know to ask about his army unit and you can't hear the accent, so you believe him."

He calls himself Sivan, but who is he really?

The only place I feel safe is in my hotel room. I'm stuck in a no-man's-land, as is the hotel where I'm staying. I've become afraid of the dark and I feel edgy and scared in both parts of Jerusalem. My shame is always with me, crushing my chest, and I know the only way to get relief is to make a complete confession. I wake up from horrible dreams in which I find body parts in my refrigerator and am about to be discovered by someone I had desperately wanted to impress.

Several days ago I came back to see Ya'akov waiting for me at the reception desk. He wouldn't take no for an answer. "Tired? At seventy you can go to bed at nine o'clock. Not feeling well? Let's go out, you'll feel better!"

I ran out of excuses, so I went along.

Ya'akov is an old friend from an earlier trip. He always makes a reappearance just when I'm about to forget him. I'm not sure why he continues to track me down, I think he simply likes the idea of having lots of friends from different countries. He's the only Israeli I know who lets me practice my Hebrew on him without showing the slightest hint of impatience. He nods, *"ken, nachon,"* "yes, right," and listens attentively, as if I had some profound wisdom to impart. He's remarkably resourceful and can take care of anything: procuring concert tickets at the last minute, finding transportation in the most unlikely places, negotiating the byzantine banking system. He's what Israelis call a *"bitzuist,"* someone who gets things done, a passionate problem solver; he radiates competence and inspires trust, so much so that I've been tempted to tell him my story any number of times. In fact, my need to confess has begun to intrude into every exchange. Sometimes it takes my last bit of strength to hold back from blurting out the whole story. I remind myself that as long as I admit nothing I can deny everything. As long as I don't give it all away, the little bits of information that I scatter along the way are harmless. But who's going to care about my half-baked account? I don't even know the truth myself. That's just it, though. I'm hoping my confessor will be astute enough to tell me what's missing and fill in the empty parts, to piece the truth together from my confused fragments of information.

"A nightclub," Ya'akov suggested, with a near-inaudible question mark. Before I had time to answer, he pushed open the door to a rowdy, dimly lit hole in the wall and made a tunnel for me through the hot, heaving bodies.

"No," I said. "No way," and fled out to the street.

Ya'akov is younger than me, but he's still too old for clubbing. "What's wrong?" he asked, following me. I regretted coming along.

In a flash I pictured all of Jerusalem out looking for a good time, while Sivan was imprisoned in a lock-up not five blocks away. He was being interrogated while I was out with Ya'akov, behaving as though Sivan had nothing to do with me. But Ya'akov left me no time to brood. He'd found a friend at the bar, his best friend, he said, and introduced us.

"You got lucky," his friend grinned. "*Mazal tov*, you landed a good one this time." Then they hustled me into the video arcade next door.

"I'm leaving," I snapped.

Ya'akov came along without protest. "What do you want to do?" he asked, his voice worried. We drifted by the boutiques and souvenir shops, letting ourselves get carried along with the crowd, past the little round café tables and the Russian street musicians and on to the flea market where Jerusalem's bright night life gives way to the twilight of drug deals and prostitution.

Sivan and I had come here after our second rendezvous in the Cardo. We were walking from the flea market into the darkness of the park where an open-air concert was playing. As we made our way through the audience, I noticed a man on the fringes, wearing a headband over his black mane and an embroidered, collarless shirt. For a moment I felt the hot giddiness of joyful renunion. I was about to call out "Gilbert" when I realized that this young man was twenty at the most and Gilbert would have to be over forty by now.

Sivan and I went to a country and western bar that he seemed to know well, along with the waitress behind the bar.

"What do you want with me?" I asked.

"I don't know," he said.

"Why me?" I repeated.

"Because you're beautiful."

No one had ever said that to me before. I wasn't at all certain he was saying what he really felt, but I liked hearing it anyway.

Sivan drank orange juice and wouldn't touch my Campari, though I encouraged him to drink it. That was the last time we went to a bar in West Jerusalem. As for restaurants, Sivan refused, with a panicky insistence, to go to them. He'd once worked in the kitchen of one of the big hotels, he said, and after he'd seen the way they treat the staff he'd decided never to eat in an Israeli restaurant again. I never learned what he ate or where. He didn't drink alcohol. He'd disappear regularly at midday and in the early evening, perhaps to pray at a mosque the way Eli went to synagogue.

That night with Ya'akov we wound up eating *burekas*, the best *burekas* in the whole country, he swore. The owner of the place welcomed him as one of his best customers. We were greeted with a torrent of words as we came through the door. "Extra cheese," Yaakov called out. "Do you want two or three?"

We sat on low stools at a small round table and ate our *burekas*, dripping with fat. The room glistened with fat, even the tiny greasy napkins, and I felt restored, sated, and freed of the need to spill out everything. There was nothing enigmatic about Ya'akov, nothing to fathom, only his good nature and effusive enthusiasm. He drank and ate and laughed all at once, with no thought of the past and no fears for the future.

My life had been heavy with secrets, complicated and uncertain until the time in the kibbutz. No one there asked me what I was doing or why I had come and I was grateful and relieved. No one cared about my background or my theories about the family scandal and the shame they'd tried to blot out.

"I have three Aryan grandparents," I told Gilbert. "But I'm a Jew."

"So what?" he said.

New lovers, we had ourselves assigned to the same work detail. When the kibbutzniks would look for us they'd shout for Romeo and Juliet. After the first few weeks, though, I kept trying to leave Gilbert at regular intervals. I've forgotten the reasons, but one of them probably involved his musical ambitions, which necessitated practicing the guitar all night.

"I can't sleep," I complained, "if you're going to practice all night. Go to the clubhouse, go to the dining room, go to the stables out back. I haven't had more than four hours sleep for weeks."

"If you're really tired, you'll sleep no matter how much noise there is," he said unimpressed.

"I've read about people going crazy because they didn't get enough sleep," I answered.

When I left him half a year later, I couldn't sleep because it was too quiet.

To stay sane I'd go down to the main gate of the kibbutz after dinner, where the old Beduin guard would take limp cucumbers or tomatoes out of his *abaya* and give them to me. They were still warm, as if he'd been cradling them in his lap for hours. He kept watch, frail, sunken, wearing a cape so large that you couldn't see the stool he was sitting on. I remember a *kaffiyeh* and a dark, sorrowful face. He tried to teach me how to catch flies, how to sit still, so that they'd perch motionless, totally unprepared, until it was too late.

Left to myself, I was preoccupied with things I'd been struggling to piece together for years despite the antagonism of those around me.

There were three women who could have given me answers, but each remained silent and stubborn in her own way—my mother with her pursed lips and withheld affection, my aunt with her anger and her sporadic torrents of words that denied accusations which no one had made, and my grandmother with her impenetrable innocence. Before I could learn to form the questions and get up the courage to ask them, two of those women died and took their secrets with them.

I was as close to my grandmother as most children are to their mothers: she brought me up. In my first, fleeting memories of security it is her face that I see, her thin, gray hair threaded with strands of black, her shapeless form under bright cotton dresses, and her hands soft, well into old age. The people I am drawn to are always like that—reticent old women who've suffered and who understand every kind of pain. You can't ask them too much because that might stir up bitter memories and cause grief. The woman who gave birth to me, my second mother, was always a stranger. She demanded love and I tried to satisfy her, but I never knew whether I succeeded. For me, home was two old people in a large, gloomy kitchen on the edge of the city, between the railway tracks and little garden plots. My grandparents lived on the second floor, in an apartment that looked like it had weathered a storm or a stroke of bad luck. Their heavy furniture and high ceilings were solidly middle-class, revealing the threadbare splendor of an earlier time.

Uncertainty, secrets, and death—these were the qualities of my childhood. And silence. A silence which sounded hollow, as if it had a false bottom. I would catch its distorted echoes in a cough or a sigh, or in the low emphasis on a particular word or name. But the subject was never named; there were no pointers to help look for what I didn't know. My grandparents simply didn't speak about Christians and Jews.

I was seven when my grandfather died; it was the first death of my life and after that we grew even closer, my grandmother and I. Then she died when I was twelve and I felt as if I'd been orphaned. It happened on a muggy summer evening and I was banished to a relative's house in the country to shield me, the child, from the heartache life can bring. I next saw her dead, laid out on a bier, and was told to take leave of her, but how do you take leave of a dead person? I curtsied and grinned to hide my embarrassment. The pain came later and never quite left. Shortly before her death, when the priest was called in, my grandmother rebelled against her lifelong silence. She refused extreme unction; she did not want a Christian burial in the grave by her husband's side; she had nothing to confess but her desire for a Jewish funeral and someone to say Kaddish for her. But she had waited too long to mutiny and no one took her late rebellion seriously. The priest assured her daughters that she had departed this earth at peace with her God.

My grandmother had often talked to me about reconciliation with the past, even up to the very last moment, but in the end there was no language for what she had kept silent for so long. For most of her life she'd been known as Beatrice, taking her place in her husband's church pew, infrequently, to be sure, but without protest. She had promised to instruct her children in that religion as best she could and had kept her own past a secret, suppressing it in every response and in every gesture. At first she had simply wanted to belong; later the fear of persecution came back to torment her. Perhaps, by the time she died, not even she knew who she really was and what she believed. Finally, when I had the right questions to ask, she was dead, and so I learned everything I had a right to know from the spiteful tongues that denounced her.

Such were the foundations of my prehistory, yet no one would confirm or deny even that much. My intuition spawned grim images, unrelenting fears which I could not escape, not even within the four walls of our house or in my own bed. I found moments of relief when hiding under the bed, but only until the next wave of dread came crashing over me.

I pondered over vague feelings which had been too ephemeral to lock into memory, watery shadows which dissolved as soon as I tried to make out their shape. Unmoored scenes would drift into my consciousness for a few seconds, unsettling and eerie, anchored by no firm knowledge nor a fixed past.

In my earliest memories there are no parents, only a grandmother for whose life I feared without knowing why and a grandfather, distant and silent, the rock that ensured our survival. Parents came later, after their wedding, three years after the war. I sat in church in a stiff white dress, between my tall, erect grandfather—always the first to step up for Communion—and my grandmother, who would slide down off the pew into a crouch rather than actually kneel. I could have been assigned to any set of parents there, my own were of so little relevance to me. My father was an emaciated gray-faced veteran of the war; my mother, a redheaded girl to whom my presence was cause for great embarrassment. Even after their wedding I continued to live with my grandparents while my parents picked me up on the weekends. I was their Sunday guest.

I learned about Jews from my father's family—half-Jews, quarter-Jews, and *Mischlingen*—and it was some time before I understood that I too was a subject of this classification. From their contemptuous expressions and disparaging remarks I concluded that they were talking about a dirty secret, a mysterious disgrace I could do nothing about, like a mark of Cain. Nevertheless, it set me apart from my cousins. To this day, my throat constricts when I feel measured up or counted out, part of a group or excluded or when I hear others talk about people halved and quartered, chopped-up into chunks, scrape those leftovers off the table, what use are bits and pieces? You'll never make a whole person out of spare parts and off-cuts. All my life I have worked to conquer the envy I feel for people who belong and are whole.

I was hardly ever able to isolate those splinters of memory from my first years, from the time before the peace and after the war; I wasn't able to hold the fragments under the light of scrutiny long enough to make sense of them. And then, one Friday afternoon in the kibbutz bathhouse, a melody shot through me like a bolt of lightning and almost split me in two. Since then I have come to believe that the joy of revelation can make you whole or drive you mad. Standing before a sink Liora, a kibbutznik, was singing *"Lecha dodi, likrat kallah,"*—"Come, my love, let us greet the Sabbath bride"—belting it out while dragging a comb through her wet hair.

"How do you know that song?" Water ran into my eyes and I left the shower steaming behind me, but I had to catch the wisp of melody from my childhood. Meaningless words and a string of notes had broken the sound barrier of forgetting. I could see a chest of drawers, a tilted mirror above it catching the morning sun in winter, some high-backed chairs around a gleaming table, and lace curtains that had seen better days. My grandmother, ancient in my eyes, her long braid of hair nimbly wound up on the back of her head, sang quietly to herself, as if she were listening for a tune she could not quite remember. Sudden pauses, the same sequence of notes over and over, and no thought of the child playing on the floor. My grandmother hummed in front of the mirror as if she were looking at someone else, as if she were tugging at the curls of a younger woman who still had reason to be vain, someone only she could see.

Another image jumped out to ambush me: Aunt Wilma, the older daughter, trying to wrest the cross from my dead grandmother's hands. But the stiff fingers would not give it up and my mother, as gentle and firm as a nun, pulled her sister away from the casket. "An abomination, a scandal," someone whispered, but there was accord in the glance the two sisters exchanged, as if they shared a secret which made them confederates despite their lifelong enmity. It wasn't until many years later that I understood what was in their eyes.

Liora looked at me with a blank expression on her face.

"I know that song you were just singing," I exclaimed happily.

"I should hope so," she said.

"Sing it again, please," I begged her, "I never heard the words before." I stood with dripping hair and a wet towel on the concrete floor of the bathhouse, afraid that the strange, melancholic melody and the image it summoned might sink back into the silent darkness before I found out more.

"What's wrong with you?" she asked. "Didn't you go to synagogue on Friday evening? Ah, I bet your parents are Communists," she said knowingly, and sang each verse. Perhaps it was the rapture on my face that made her sing.

Later that evening, after the Sabbath candles had been lit and fresh, white tablecloths were spread on the long dining tables, Liora took me up to her room. The sun had set and on the stone houses and farm buildings a stillness lay so complete that it seemed work had stopped forever. Liora's room looked like a young girl's sanctuary, dressed up with dried flowers, knickknacks and little pictures. But Liora was a few years older than I; she had already completed her military service and returned to the kibbutz to wait for a man to love.

"This is your evening," she said. "You can look at anything you want and listen to my records and I won't ask any questions."

She put one record after another on her cheap little phonograph and looked at me eagerly, hoping for a repetition of the afternoon's performance and the renewed satisfaction of being the one to call forth my emotions. But the crack in my memory had already closed and we both waited, increasingly disappointed, as each new Israeli dance tune led further and further away from the past.

"This one, listen, I really like it." Liora laid her hand on my arm. "We used to do this when I lived in the children's house. My mother was still alive and she always liked to sing this song."

But I was distracted, waiting for a note to emerge from the

depths. I thought about Gilbert and wondered whether he was with the new Irish volunteer. I was restless and didn't want to hear any more of Liora's records.

She raised the stylus in the middle of a sentimental Yiddish song and suddenly I felt ashamed. I was too immature to become friends with Liora, too self-absorbed. After many years I still feel ashamed when I think of her. She offered me friendship and I didn't take the time nor make the effort to listen to her. *"Shabbat Shalom,"* she said at the door, in a quiet, disappointed voice, and from then on I avoided her. I can still see her, short and plump with curly hair and a brave smile, her hand on the door knob.

No one in Jerusalem knows my real name, the one I was baptised with, Hildegard. It's my other grandmother's name, my father's mother. Only Channa-Frieda knows it—I'm always open with her—but she still calls me Devorah. "If it makes you happy," she said. "Anyway it suits you." I chose it myself when I renounced my baptism and the other Christian sacraments of my childhood and completed the conversion my grandmother had only hinted at. But my old name still appears in my passport and in all my other documents. Choosing the name Devorah was always an act of impertinence, probably aimed at my country's extreme sense of order. After all, what would happen if we all just took whatever name we liked?

Sometimes I also use my grandmother's maiden name and then I'm my own woman—a new name and a new person unhampered by other people's preconceptions: Devorah's afraid of nothing, not even afraid of not belonging. Devorah's courageous;

she has no past to be ashamed of, in fact, she has no past at all. She has no age, even the information in her passport is out of date. She invents her own history and personality. One day I might need to drop her too, but for the moment I like her, I'm proud of her, and willing to take responsibility for her mistakes.

Devorah doesn't speak German, either. She knows German but she's just not interested in speaking it. Her hair is a half-tone darker than it was in Hildegard's youth, hiding the strands of gray. And she dresses a little younger than her age, so no one would guess how old she is. I like looking at her reflection in store windows and in the eyes of people walking my way. Devorah is the woman I always wanted to be.

Since I was a child I've always liked dressing up and inventing other lives for myself. "The child lies for no reason at all," they said, "a disturbing character trait."

"Where are your parents?" they asked me in the Schlosspark of the Imperial Villa, when I was looking for the exit, lost but not frightened, quite self-possessed in fact.

"I don't have any parents," I said. "My mother was deported when I was small and my father lives in Italy. I've only seen him once, he's very famous."

It was partially true in some essential way, like many of my inventions. Perhaps Martha was my real mother, and that's why I look like her and why she watched over me from inside the frame of her portrait, from high up at first, in the dark hallway near the kitchen door. Later I grew level with her and began to speak to her. I didn't actually ask about her until much later.

"Who's the woman in the picture?"

"Martha, a cousin of mine," my grandmother said.

"Is she dead?"

"We don't know," she said evasively. I knew not to ask any more questions.

Once, at the table, Aunt Wilma peered at me searchingly. I must have been five or six years old at the time. "She's getting to look more and more like Martha," she said to her mother. "Don't you think so?" Obviously distressed, my grandmother dismissed the observation.

Long before I knew her story, Martha's portrait lived in my imagination. It was my property, my older sister, my intimate friend: a narrow face against a dark background, the white lace of an old-fashioned dress, amber hair, slanting brown eyes not quite looking at the viewer, not really looking at anyone, not even the brush-wielding painter. Her gaze traveled through him and was lost in a myopic distance. Still, I was convinced that her eyes fixed on me when I wasn't looking her way and I tried to catch her at it.

"She always wore clothes like that," my grandmother said. "Long skirts, made of velvet and lace. She liked being noticed."

Whenever the doorbell rang I thought it might be her. One day I'd see her standing at the door, I was sure of it.

"If she's still alive," my grandmother said, with bitter doubt in her voice.

It pained me to know so little about Martha. How old was she in the picture? What was the room like where she was sitting? What was she thinking at that moment? What did she feel for the painter facing her? I talked to her and practiced her expression in the mirror, wondering what it might mean. She was the key to something I didn't understand and couldn't name. Her mother had been my great-great-aunt, I had been told. But she stayed young while I grew older, becoming the big sister I didn't have. We shared the loneliness of the dark, quiet apartment, and while my grandmother grew ill and wasted away, Martha continued to look out at us with the equanimity of timeless youth. I admired her with the fervor of a precocious child who lives most of her life in dreams. I sought comfort from her when I suffered a defeat and with her help I turned insults into compliments.

I learned about her story piece by piece over a period of years, but I'm still trying to find out how her life ended. I've never given up the hope that she might still be alive. I see signs of her everywhere, in faces I meet, in stories people tell me, in old hands on the bus grasping shopping bags. I've long held the suspicion that she might well have had very different features from the dreamy melancholy look her artist husband put into the oil painting. However she looked, her presence taught me that the real power in my life was my ability to imagine things and make them happen, just because I wanted them so badly. From Martha's portrait I learned that desire can transform reality.

After my grandmother's death the picture disappeared. Wilma took it away with her, but Martha had become so deeply ingrained in me that I no longer needed her image to keep her alive. I moved to my parents' house and shut myself in my room with my defiant dreams. There was no one with whom I could talk about Martha but I studied the adults carefully and learned how they lied, how they disguised clues, altered events, and completely glided over certain years. If I asked them about these things, they simply didn't answer.

"Where are we from?" I asked my mother, making my question sound casual.

"We're Austrian," she said, and it sounded like a reprimand.

"Why isn't grandmother's side of the family buried in the cemetery?"

"They're in Bohemia and we can't go there."

I didn't dare ask any more, didn't dare repeat what I'd heard in my father's family's house, that something was wrong with us, that Wilma was a whore and Grandmother a fraud. All you had to do was look at us, you could see for yourself. But what was it that they saw? For years I felt guilty of some offense I couldn't possibly have committed.

My grandmother was rarely mentioned after she died and no one talked about the time euphemistically referred to as "the bad years." My parents had no past, only a future for which they worked and saved. In their house my early memories were stifled altogether. But my grandmother had refused to call me Hildegard, saying it was bad luck to name a child for a living person. So she called me Bienchen, little bee, Devorah in Hebrew, and I never forgot it. When I reclaimed my childhood name I also became the biblical Deborah, the prophet and the judge.

"My name is Devorah," I told Sivan, but he never called me by my name.

"And mine is Sivan, but my friends call me Mike or Number Seven. You can choose the one you like best."

Maybe he's picked this particular name just for me, along with the rest of his identity.

"My father was a Catholic who went to church every Sunday. I play the organ," he said with a touch of pride.

"Where was your father born?"

"In Jerusalem."

"And your grandfather?"

"Turkey."

That's all he told me. Religion? He wasn't interested. "I don't go to church," he claimed, "I avoid it." I'd act dumb and a little rude, just to provoke him. "I don't care whether you go to church, I'm only asking out of curiosity. And your family? What happened in Turkey?"

He shrugged. "I don't really know the details."

After half an hour Anahita had told me all about her parents and a young girl I once met in her shop introduced herself as the third generation after the genocide.

Sometimes I tried to tell Sivan about myself but he was indifferent, preoccupied, and I sensed an aggressive impatience, as if he resented everything that excluded him. Still, when we were actually together there were no uncertainties and no mistrust. From the very beginning, there was a profound intimacy between us, pure and free of doubt.

"To me it feels," he said, on the second day as we stood looking over the Mount of Olives, "as if I've known you all my life."

Below us lay the Muslim cemetery with its desolate gravestones, plastic bags and dirty rags caught in the branches of the carob trees.

We talked about our hopes. Sivan lit cigarettes for me and the wind blew out his matches. We'd touch each other unexpectedly and then briefly hold our breath. We acted casually, as if we were sitting next to one another entirely by chance, but we were both a little frightened. I don't believe we were lying then; lies don't permit so much intimacy. Our bodies' walls seemed to dissolve every time we touched, although we were shy and careful with each other. He was so young, he had little to talk about—brothers and sisters, friends, drives to the Dead Sea in his uncle's car, hashish in water pipes, a love which ended while it was still painful, a woman he followed to Australia and his return, because he would always come back here, to Mount Zion.

"And you?"

"I'm divorced, like everyone my age. And as for old boyfriends, they're not important. They're like those rags down there, I don't remember where they came from and don't really want to talk about them, not because it's painful, but because it doesn't matter."

I didn't tell him that I fell in love for the first time in this city, in these streets. I was twenty years younger and wandered hand in hand with Gilbert through the souk and along the city walls—there were no sidewalks and the narrow roads were piled high with rubble from the Six Day War. Somewhere behind the stone walls a baby was screaming and maybe it was him.

The wind grew cool in the west, but at the foot of the city wall the sun still lit up the shrubs.

"I know every square meter of the Old City," he said, "every gust of wind. Once I went to visit family in Texas and I should have stayed there but it was too foreign. I ran away."

I've felt more at home in every city that I've ever visited than I have in my birthplace, but I didn't tell Sivan about that. It would've opened up my complicated story which I prefer not to talk about in this country. Devorah can only exist if the story stays hidden under wraps.

Below, the white stones of the city wall soaked up the evening sun and glowed deep yellow as if illuminated from within. As the wind ruffled the stiff grass we moved closer together.

"Excuse me," he said, "may I ask you something?"

"Yes," I said, full of curiosity.

Sometimes, when he turned toward me, there was a clumsy gentility in his movements, as if my presence were a prize and any extra generosities I might bestow a bonus that only increased my value.

"May I kiss you?" he asked.

I must have laughed and said yes.

In the days and weeks that followed I began to squirrel away the image of his changeable face into my store of memories: his look of surprise, the small scar under his left brow, his mouth, which could suddenly, without the slightest provocation, age with bitterness. But at that moment his features, darkened with desire, showed a new aspect, a sweet sadness and the naked yearning of a child who has forgotten his inhibitions. That was how he looked every time he leaned over me, yielding and gentle, as if I were a coveted, delicate object.

In the dim light of the setting sun the stone walls began to glow, revealing fine red veins in the rock. The dome of the Omar Mosque burned in a gold blaze, while thick shadows pushed their way up the winding alleyways. When we stood up and shook the grass from our clothes and hair, the cold wind tore through my hair.

"How do I look?" I asked.

"Beautiful. Happy."

Sivan walked with me to the central bus station in West Jerusalem. It was the only time he voluntarily went beyond his turf. He watched as the bus backed out of the station into the night, into the western suburbs, into the mountains where he wouldn't go. The next day I left the kibbutz in the hills outside Jerusalem and moved into a hotel in the center of the city.

From that day on we spent at least a few hours together every evening. After all his offers to show me around, there were endless places where Sivan wouldn't go. Much of West Jerusalem and the Old City soon became off-limits for us.

"I don't want anyone to see us together," he said. "Armenians love to gossip. It's a small, incestuous community and when a rumor starts to make the rounds you never know where it'll end."

So all that was left to us were the two slopes that separated West Jerusalem from the Old City, from Mount Zion to the Dung Gate and the Hinnom Valley. Sivan picked figs and peeled them for me so their pink fruit shone moist; he rubbed lavender and rosemary between his palms and held them up to my nose saying, "Smell how good that is." Sometimes he found stones broken into small, uniform cubes with surfaces so smooth they seemed polished. "They use stones like these to make mosaics," he explained. Along the wall, in the shade of its ruins, solitary, pale blue flowers struggled to survive the summer heat. Sivan stuck them in my hair and in the neck of my blouse. Scorched as it was, Mount Zion became a feast for my senses. Sivan regretted that it wasn't spring when everything was in bloom, and searched hard for the English names for the flowers and fruits he gave me to smell, to taste, to admire. On our walks across the rocky slopes we were always on the lookout for secluded places where we could kiss unobserved, and we soon found a favorite site in the shade of an olive tree. The only person who could see us was the Palestinian watchman at Sultan's Pool, but he soon lost interest.

Sivan courted me in an old-fashioned, chivalrous way and it amused me. At any moment he would break out into boyish exuberance, although there was always a trace of arrogance in his ardor. But he demanded nothing of me, no pretense, no subservience, and I was content to feel adored and trusting.

"Let's go to the beach in Caesarea or Tel Aviv," I suggested.

"We can't."

"Why not?"

"I have to work."

"Why aren't you at university?"

He grasped things quickly and always knew how to solve a problem although sometimes he was cocksure. I didn't understand his humor though, nor his way of switching off the world outside him. He'd act as if he hadn't heard certain things I'd said, and it was useless to repeat a question that he didn't want to answer. He asked about me with a polite formality that obliged me to act in the same way. We didn't talk about the many things that lovers usually do; even in moments of intimacy, Sivan would pull up an unyielding drawbridge that fended off the question, "Tell me, who are you, really?" From the beginning, I saw the inconsistencies in his behavior—his capacity for absolute devotion on the one hand, and the reserve with which he rebuffed me, on the other. I was never entirely certain where I stood with him and now it is this uncertainty which pains me the most.

"I'd like to study languages," Sivan said. "I'd like to be a teacher."

"Well? Why don't you give it a try?"

"It's not that easy."

That's what he said when a conversation was over.

He worked for UNICEF, he told me. They had recruited him to do reporting for a film project, a documentary on the West

Bank and Gaza. They had chosen him because he knew languages and was neutral, neither Arab nor Jewish.

"I'm their interpreter and also the audio engineer. I'm the only one who knows how to use the equipment."

"How long is the project going to last?"

"I don't know."

"What are you going to do when it's finished?"

"I'll cross that bridge when I get to it. I get four hundred dollars a day," he said proudly. "And they made me study English, an intensive language course for three months."

"And before that? How did you know English?"

"From the tourists."

"And Hebrew?"

"From the streets, I just picked it up. I don't have an accent, you can't tell me apart from an Israeli."

When I spoke Hebrew he laughed so hard he doubled up, mimicking every mistake in my intonation until I finally gave up and went back to English.

"And your boss is American?"

"European."

He never knew when they'd need him and he'd get restless in the early evening. "I have to make a call to find out when I have to be there tomorrow." Then he'd disappear for an hour or so.

"Don't they have a schedule?" I asked him. "Why do they wait until the evening before telling you what they're going to be doing?"

"You're always asking questions," he said. "There isn't always a reason for everything, some things are just the way they are. You think too much, you know. Start listening to your instincts."

"It's a European film team," I countered. "They don't work according to their feelings from one day to the next. How long have you been working for them?"

"A while."

"It's been weeks since we met. A documentary doesn't take that long."

"We sit around and drink coffee and talk. Then we drive somewhere, to Bethlehem or Hebron, and we interview people."

If he was stingy with details about his timetable he was very free with anecdotes he picked up along the way. He told me about Jews who were buying up Arab land, about Palestinian students who refused to use an interpreter even though their English didn't make any sense. His stories were always trivial, routine, and I wasn't able to form any coherent picture of what he actually did. Later he added a new story about his cousin's forthcoming marriage and all the things that had to be done to the house before the couple could move in. He was working every night almost until dawn, he had to be there at nine, ten at the latest, and was dead tired the next day.

I could choose to believe him or not, but I couldn't ask any more questions. Somehow everything seemed to ring true, but a little false at the same time. Occasionally one of his friends would show up in the role of assistant, grinning, as if they were both duping me, and Sivan would have to leave with him immediately on an urgent assignment.

There was no telephone number or address where I could reach him. He was always waiting at our usual meeting place, although I didn't know which direction he came from and he'd leave after taking me as far as Zion Square. Still, it never once occurred to me that one day he simply wouldn't be there.

I decided to ask Ya'akov what he knew about this UNICEF

camera team, but I couldn't track him down. I found his friend Omri, the one who'd congratulated me on making such a splendid match, in a pizzeria on Shammai Street. He was at the counter, drinking a cup of Turkish coffee and chain smoking.

"Have you seen Ya'akov?" I asked. "I've been looking for him for several days."

He shrugged his shoulders. "Not today. Maybe he's got a new woman."

"Have you heard anything about a UNICEF documentary in the Old City, going on for weeks now?"

"Nonsense," Omri declared. "Israel wouldn't allow it. Who's been telling you such stories?"

"Oh, I just heard it." Then we talked about the situation, as it's called, and about the Intifada in particular. It was so easy to talk to him. He trusted me and just assumed I was on his side.

What was my crime? Not knowing? Being slow to learn the rules of the Middle Eastern game? Not acting on my suspicions when I could smell Sivan's fear in Jewish West Jerusalem? "We're living in a state of war," everyone told me. "Not a week goes by without a stabbing, a bomb on a bus, Molotov cocktails hurled at windshields, burning tires, every day another casualty." Sivan sympathized with the other side and I was too green to know that his allegiance made him my enemy.

I took for my summer lover a man forbidden to me—that was my real offense, the crime for which I would have to be punished. And now I'm fair game: the men in the souk size me up frankly, the way they look at whores and scrawl their message to the soldiers across storefronts: "We fuck your women."

I spent the first Sabbath morning alone in my hotel. The

street below was deserted, not a single car or bus for miles. I wrote letters, did my laundry, and was happy to be by myself for a whole day. I sent the hotel attendant away with his fresh towels, cleaning fluids and dusters. "I'll make my own bed," I said.

"Where are you from?" he asked. "What is your religion?"

He had burnished skin and the most beautiful black eyes I had ever seen. He looked at me with bottomless sorrow and asked whether he could come back later to talk about a problem. My response was sympathetic.

"And you?" I asked, dumb and ignorant, as if a Jew would be changing dirty linens on a Saturday morning.

"Can't you tell?" he said.

I had been in Jerusalem for less than a week and I came from a milieu in which people didn't talk about their differences—in fact, they strove to reassure each other that there were none and that they were, in any case, irrelevant. I thought I was supposed to ignore the things that made people different.

"I'm a little bit of everything," he said. "My mother's Jewish and my father's Palestinian."

"Is that difficult?" I asked.

"Very bad. When I come back I'll tell you about it."

When he returned he told me a far-fetched story which even I couldn't believe, about a German mother, a rich Jordanian father, and how he had been disinherited for wanting to marry a young Israeli woman. After their engagement she had died in an automobile accident. Since then he'd been living as an outcast with an aunt in a Jerusalem suburb, sentenced to a life of poverty and the disgrace of his menial job. Since then, not a single day of happiness or love, only misery.

"Would you do something for me?" he asked.

He needed an affidavit to travel to Europe, a letter to a Jordanian official so that he could leave the country.

"I thought you lived in Israel?"

"Yes, but I have a Jordanian passport."

"How come?"

At that point he nudged me back toward the bed. "Just half an hour and I'll go," he said, as if I owed him something. "Don't be so coy," he pulled at my shirt. "What's wrong with you? Just half an hour."

I gave him a shove in the direction of the door. He was slight and a little unsure of himself. "Get the hell out of here!" I yelled. "Right now!" Then I went down to the reception desk. "I'm afraid of him," I lied. "What if he has a pass key, what if he comes back?"

"What did he look like?" the young woman asked.

"Short," I said, "thin, big eyes."

"Good-looking?" Her smile annoyed me.

"I don't know, I didn't notice."

"Did anything happen?"

"No, but it could, the next time."

"I'll tell the manager."

I liked the rush of power and strength. I'd show him—he could kiss his job good-bye.

Sitting in an armchair near the reception desk, a dark young woman with a mass of black curly hair was watching me. If the bellboy hadn't propositioned me, I would never have met Nurit.

"Is there something about me that provoked him?" I asked her and Ada, her friend at the reception desk.

"It's something else entirely," Nurit interrupted. "But it's political, I can't explain it in two minutes. Are you really afraid of him?" She gave me a hard look. I've seen it many times since—a look that induces discomfort and a need to confess, and I've learned how effective it is.

She guessed at the truth: I didn't feel threatened; on the contrary, I felt vindictive and powerful, with justice on my side. It was good to feel that way for once. There were two classes of people in the hotel and he had forgotten that. I wouldn't have insisted on the distinction if he hadn't disregarded it. But Nurit made me alarmed at the self-righteous pleasure I took in my position.

That evening the manager—a mustachioed Palestinian, solemn and remote—stepped my way as I was going upstairs to my room.

"Did you want to make a complaint?" he asked. Before his reproachful eyes I could find no justification and no explanation. Just look at you, his eyes said, your arms, your neckline, your belly and hips, everything shamelessly on show. Your bare legs in high-heeled sandals, your clothes black and red, the colors of temptation, whore's colors. What do you expect? Respect?

"The man has a family, he comes here every day from the West Bank. He hasn't been here very long. He's never done anything like this before." I saw contempt in the manager's expression, but his voice was calm. There was no overt criticism, not one unseemly word for the guest, but his eyes called me foolish. You're a silly single woman, they said, and everything about you is begging to get laid. Except that the moment a man responds to your call, you turn sweet and demure. You'd destroy a man's living just like that, just because you feel like it. You can protest your innocence all you like but I know you're a whore.

The next day I moved out. I couldn't bear his accusing presence and his disdain.

Nurit shrugged her shoulders when I told her. "They judge women harshly, their own, too. There's nothing we can do about it, that's why I dress the way I do." Nurit always covered her arms and knees, but she strode through Jerusalem like an exotic princess cutting a path through the masses.

And in the evening, once the Sabbath had ended and I met Sivan, I told him what had happened, recounting the story as an entertaining anecdote, over and done with. But Sivan didn't take it lightly; he didn't think the story was trivial. His hostile eyes squinted at some distant point and he punished me with iciness, walking ahead with quick steps.

"What did I do?" I asked.

"It's not surprising that we think foreign women are idiots. Look at the way they behave." He was doing his best to choose neutral words.

The joy of having Sivan close and my desire for his touch was gone. With him, nothing was simple or inconsequential.

"Do you think I'd just sleep with anybody?" I asked.

"No, I don't." He seemed to be defending himself against an accusation only he could hear.

But my behavior troubled him. In the beginning he often looked at me adoringly, like a rare specimen of some strange species—me, a woman who traveled alone, rented a car and insisted on visiting the West Bank, who drove along the Syrian border in full view of the army, who came and went as she pleased. But then he grew jealous and began to comment on my dress and my movements; he looked for signs of another man and interrogated me.

"You smoked all those cigarettes?" He counted twelve butts in the ashtray. "You never smoke that many, someone else was with you." He spoke through a clenched jaw and I sensed his barely contained violence.

"Maybe I gave a soldier a ride, I don't remember."

"I told you not to pick up strange men, it's dangerous."

"Soldiers aren't rapists," I answered angrily.

He was beginning to love me and hate me with a tortuous greed. If I'd gotten involved with him so easily maybe I was doing the same thing with other men behind his back. I was a foolish woman whom he loved and whose honor had become his. He examined a scratch on my shoulder with a crazed expression, seeking evidence of an interloper. He pushed me away and stalked off, only to return and brood over his despair. I couldn't help him. After all, I hardly knew him.

III

I walk up and down Jaffa Road several times a day. As a result, I'm learning how to distinguish barely perceptible shades of the spectrum, to catch the swift transition from dusk to darkness, to tell the difference between an Arab and a Jew. As you approach the Old City, the houses become older and shabbier; their blue-painted shutters are made of wood and their wrought iron balconies have not been closed in by modern sliding blinds; their doors open right onto the street. Some shops seem to have no doors at all—the street trickles through the entrance to fade into windowless gloom. Here is where east and west mingle and merge and you can't be sure which part of the city you're looking at. Bagels stacked on wooden poles grow cold and hard as rocks next to aluminum trays of tahini and hummus. The man reaching across the counter to hand me a pita with falafel might be Palestinian or Polish or Moroccan. I wouldn't care one way or the other were I not continually made to feel that I should and that my indifference can kill.

This spot, this short stretch of Jaffa Road, is the realm of transitions where tributaries from the Old City flow into the New. Here—on these two or three blocks ending at the old beggar's post in Zion Square, and the string of cafés where tourists drink mint tea under sun umbrellas advertising Dubek cigarettes and Maccabi beer—is where Adam prowls for foreign women and Sivan tries out his languages. Here is where I need my suspicion most, as I sit in a greasy little café with the crumbs and paper cup a predecessor left behind.

The setting sun throws a ruby-red shaft of light into the glass lemonade container by the door; behind me, in the shadows, a humming refrigerator cools soft drinks, yogurt, and goat's cheese. For weeks now I've been living on falafel, yogurt, and coffee. Closer to the entrance, still in bright daylight, a man dips pita bread into a dish of hummus. We take each other's measure and come simultaneously to a positive conclusion, smiling at each other briefly. As he gets up, he voices a soft *"Shalom"* in my direction. A moment ago, sitting at his table he could've been my next-door neighbor. But now, as he stands in the doorway, a dark figure against the sun, his gaze has something provocative in it, from which I turn away in discomfort. He seems to weigh whether to join me at my table, ask who I am and where I come from, just to see what might come of it. Is there a signal in his look, a clue I am missing? My insecurity turns me against him. He sits back down to drink a glass of Turkish coffee, all the while keeping me in his line of vision. He was simply ordering his coffee, I sigh with relief. But then a twinge shoots through me: is this the man they've put on my tail, I wonder, is he just playing a little game with me?

I straighten up to stare back at him and he grins.

The city is a minefield. Every step I take is loaded with fear and anticipation, each one could herald the end of my freedom. Day after day, at every corner, the thought that I might run into Sivan or someone carrying a message from him sends my heart leaping up to my throat and drives beads of sweat out through my pores. Then I take a second look, only to see a stranger with the same shirt or walk or haircut, and after that the exhaustion, the dizziness, as if my blood had sunk down to my toes and brought my heart to a sudden stop. And I wander along Jaffa Road with a hope that I hide from myself and a desire that I deny.

When you know nothing and fear nothing a street is just a way to reach your destination, a restaurant is simply a place to eat, and a park means a little shade where you can survive the hottest hours of the day. Before I met Sivan, I often used to sit in Independence Park during the midday heat: If you're lucky, you can find a cool patch of pine shade speckled with sunlight. The sparse scorched grass is strewn with broken glass and garbage, but the glass shards, ground into the ground, light up and sparkle when hit by a ray of sun. Then Nurit declared the park unsafe, even during the day.

"It makes me uncomfortable," she said, when I suggested we meet there. But she came anyway and looked around warily.

"No, no, we can't stay here, absolutely not. Look at those two characters over there, they're coming our way. No, not here either. This place is creepy, can't you feel it? It's dangerous."

"Then let's go over to Mamilla, it's always quiet there," I said.

"God help us, that's even worse, unless you're looking for hashish. The men there are all pimps, you know."

Sivan and I often met in the park. It was the only place in West Jerusalem where he felt safe, where you'd meet more Arabs and foreigners than Jews. But I felt uncomfortable there at night and urged him to find a spot where we wouldn't be followed by prying, lecherous eyes. We usually solved the dilemma by going deeper into the park, finding cover under the thick overhanging bushes. After I rented a car, we'd sometimes drive over to Liberty Bell Park in West Jerusalem late at night. There, Orthodox Jewish boys played basketball while their mothers watched from benches. Little children jumped up and down on trampolines rigged with safety nets.

Sometimes Sivan found a couple of friends there. They seemed to be waiting for him behind the park fence. He'd motion them to come over, exchange a few quiet words so quickly and casually that I couldn't even identify which language they were speaking, and sometimes small objects or a note changed hands.

The day I rented the car, he swung the key triumphantly over his head, and signaled to his friends as if it were a trophy. I dismissed the gesture, thinking that when it comes to cars, people in this country are very childish.

A few of his friends introduced themselves; none of them was over thirty and some seemed much younger.

"Yossi," said one. His eyes were narrowly spaced in an alert, intelligent face that was framed by a shock of black hair. In fact, he showed up so often and in so many different places that I suspected he had a twin.

"My real name is Yassin, Dir Yassin, have you heard of it? There was a massacre there. I live in the Cardo." He said he was a Christian Arab and explained that he'd been named after a

Jerusalem village where the entire population had been murdered during the 1948 Israeli Independence War.

Only slightly surprised I asked, "You live in the Cardo? I thought only Jews lived there."

"I'm Mike's assistant," he said, grinning. Frequently, I asked questions that they didn't seem to hear. And none of them knew Sivan by any other name but Mike.

"So, how is he?" Yassin-Yossi asked, indicating Sivan with his chin. "A good Armenian, no?"

He was mocking me and slipping me a message, too. He knew that I wouldn't hear his warning now but I'd remember it much later.

The rest of Sivan's friends would stand around, eyeing me.

"Do all your friends live in East Jerusalem?" I asked Sivan, searching, fishing for information.

"No, there are others, just not many. The tall one who didn't say a word is Israeli, and there are a couple more."

But I never met them.

Eventually, I refused to go to Liberty Bell Park. I didn't want to meet anymore of Sivan's friends either, I finally said. I didn't like the way they looked at me, like a lump of unkosher meat. Sivan agreed, and we went back to spending our time alone.

Then one day, out of the blue, he said we had to meet his friends. "It's important, there's a problem, they're counting on me."

We waited in the darkness of a West Jerusalem parking lot. Three men approached our car and Sivan got out. They spoke quietly, in Arabic, and then a fourth, stationed on the side-walk, gave a signal. Together we walked over to Jaffa Road and continued toward the pedestrian mall. For a long time we stood in silence, enveloped in a vague apprehension. I looked at Sivan questioningly, but he'd forgotten I was there. His attention was focused on some fixed point in the distance that was invisible to me. In a moment the tension eased and I understood that our watch was over.

"Let's get something to eat," one of the friends said, and suddenly they were speaking English and Hebrew. It was late, past eleven, but the cafés and souvenir shops were still open. Long-haired kids from the youth hostels were draped over the concrete benches, Israeli men with their army crew cuts were on the lookout for pretty women, and Jerusalem's nightlife went on, gentle and peaceful.

We got falafel at one of the kiosks and sat down outside. A young English girl caught Sivan's attention and I watched and listened while he said the same things to her that he'd said to me when we met, the same feeble jokes that I'd tried not to hold against him, the same compliments, as if he were giving me a repeat performance of our first day together. This time it was with a younger woman, who responded with more enthusiasm.

"I'm Amy," she said, shaking long, shiny hair. "Do you want to meet tomorrow?"

"We'll probably run into each other," he said, unpredictably cool. He motioned to the rest of us, "Let's go." Amy gave me a brief, startled look; it obviously hadn't occurred to her that I was with this group.

Sivan put his arm around my waist and kissed me, right in the middle of the street, but I felt no sense of triumph or reassurance. Sadness had worked its way into my bones. That night I decided to put an end to our ridiculous romance.

For almost a week I avoided the Old City. I visited Frieda and spent one afternoon with Nurit in a garden café in Ein Kerem. But anxiety robbed me of my composure. I forced myself not to think about Sivan. Nurit gave me a suspicious look. "What's wrong with you?"

I decided to visit Tel Aviv for a few days instead of just sitting around waiting for I didn't know what to happen.

When I got back to the hotel that evening, the night clerk handed me an envelope. A passport photo fell into my hands as I tore it open, and a pair of large, startled eyes stared up from the flat surface. "Remember me?" was printed on the back in block letters. I fingered the photo, unable to form a clear thought. I wanted to go to him. The struggle to put him out of my mind gave way to an urgent desire to see him now, immediately, tonight.

When I went to the Old City the next afternoon, he was waiting for me just as if we'd made a date.

"I knew you'd come!" he yelled, and was so high-spirited and happy that I couldn't maintain the cool, distant reception I'd planned. We walked alongside the wall to the spot where we'd first kissed.

"I flirt with other girls," he said. "Once I even made three dates for the same afternoon. It's a game, but you—with you it's something different."

It wasn't as if I'd never heard this kind of thing before, or that I even believed him—it just didn't matter whether he lied or not. When we were together his affection seemed generous and warm, entirely free of calculation. I detected not one false note in his tenderness and his touch. What do I know about his culture? I told myself. Maybe, in his own way, he is telling the truth.

Was he a honey trap? The very question makes me squirm,

ANNA MITGUTSCH

tarred and feathered as I am with the shame of the collaborator. I see contempt in the eyes of the hotel clerk, reproach in the eyes of the chamber maid. Mocking eyes, vicious and lecherous, eyes that despise me in my crazy flight back and forth across the city. They know me, those eyes. They know my secrets and how pitiful I really am, with my longing for adventure and my pathetic disguise of youth—simply a ridiculous figure that didn't grow up. I see those eyes in every man I meet; I challenge his stare boldly but then I'm on the run again—out into the burning street, past the fortress-like post office and down the slope to the Old City wall, blinding in the heat like a white, chalky cliff.

When I used to come to Jerusalem with Gilbert on Saturdays, the approach to the wall was blocked by acacias and thick gorse bushes. In the years since, the weeds were cleared and newly planted palm trees grew to spread their shade. Indeed, while I was away Jerusalem shed its rubble and barbed wire and emerged shining, majestic. Pale stone settlements now stretch along the high mountain ridges like bony vertebrae, tracing the road winding up from the coastal plain. At dawn, the Old City lies under a milky veil, a delicate blue; by noon the wall is bleached to an intense glare and shimmer, which softens in the late afternoon. The sun draws out blood-colored veins in the stone while gouging shadows into its smoothness. And as darkness steals through the narrow streets of the Old City, the Dome of the Rock flares, a bright beacon trimmed with strands of gold glittering from the church steeples. Twilight wanes, and before Jerusalem settles into night the sky turns blue again, more turquoise than at daybreak.

Lights twinkle across the city, from the squat Arab villages in the West Bank, to the Mount of Olives, to the distant shore of the Mediterranean. Out of the souk's alleys the shadows come creeping, turning the mulberry trees into large black hands that grab at the patches of grass. The wind touches the slanting pines like an ardent lover, tender and patient; it strokes their whispering leaves with long fingers. And away in the distance, the mountains of Moab and round hollows of the desert fade in the night's thick blackness.

A few days ago I spent the whole afternoon in the souk in a shop laden with embroidered Beduin dresses and scarves, kilims and blankets. I don't know why I stayed so long. Occasionally you meet a person who reminds you of someone from the past, and so it was with the shopkeeper who offered me a glass of Turkish coffee. He didn't try to make a sale or seduce me; he only wanted to talk, and I wanted to listen.

"You're not in a hurry," he said, "I can see by your walk."

I sat down on a pile of authors.

"Not many tourists now, not since the Intifada. A few hours feel like a whole day, it goes so slowly."

I made a sound of sympathy.

"You know, we're a lot alike, the Jews and Palestinians," he went on. "It's just that no one wants to see it. If a Frenchman moves to America he becomes an American. The same goes for a German or almost anyone else. But we Jews and Palestinians have our roots here and we can't pull them up and plant them somewhere else. It doesn't matter how long we're away, we just can't settle anywhere, we'd shrivel up and die. In our hearts we're always here, in Jerusalem."

He was the first person I met in Jerusalem who said "we."

The verandah at the Quarter Café in the Jewish Quarter is one of my favorite spots for passing the afternoon. Today I am waiting to meet one Frau Wittrich, a tour guide who once lived in the city where I grew up. Two Russian immigrants below play "Jerusalem the Golden" on their violins over and over again. Three feet away a rapacious creeper is smothering a cedar. Both grew out of the ruins of a synagogue, or maybe it was a mosque or a church. One way or another, there's nothing left of it now but a stone arch, which frames a view of the Al-Aqsa Mosque. I can see the heavy stone blocks of Silwan on one side of the valley and the round arches of the Hotel Intercontinental on the other.

When I tire of the view, I turn back to the shady tables under the arbor. The people seated have a reason to be here, in Jerusalem rather than, say, Paris or Rome. They bring their scattered histories and tangled stories and expect to make sense of them, to find some resolution. They come here with expectations they would never direct toward Paris or Rome. They pin their hopes on this city; surely its sweep and significance will infuse their own narrow histories with greater meaning and coherence.

At the next table, four Americans are arguing in loud voices. "I'm telling you, this rabbi is a saint," a gigantic man with an unkempt beard and swiveling eyes pounds on the table. "He could just as well be the messiah. I used to visit him every year in New Jersey, until he moved here." His companions are giving him tough competition, though, and it's anyone's guess who'll outscream the others. The one with the loudest voice turns out to be a visiting professor from Los Angeles who sings a chorus of praise for Orthodoxy. Thank God, her three daughters have all married good men in Israel.

On the promenade leading to the Jaffa Gate, Jodie, an American, sets out her photographs of the Western Wall. She also takes close-up pictures—keepsakes—of the little folded scraps of paper on which Jewish supplicants from all over the world write their prayers, then squeeze them into the chinks of the wall. Millions of wishes sealed with tears and prayer, and above them the melancholic cry of Muslims at worship.

"When the Messiah comes, that'll be the end of the mosque," Jodie says. She has secured herself a box seat with her camera and tripod. She comes from Poughkeepsie, a place where she never really felt alive.

"I can't stand America anymore," she declares. "It's all too shallow and empty. Here, life has meaning and focus, here I know what my purpose is." Whenever she leaves her post for a time, Josh, her neighbor, watches over her pictures. Josh, from Oregon, sells silver jewelry set with semiprecious stones and manages to be silent in two languages. He gives terse replies and doesn't bargain with customers. In any case, money isn't so important that he would ever lose his composure over it; he sits on the steps and meditates.

Of course, I also like the Via Dolorosa and watching the pilgrims, their hands bound with rosaries, working their way up the steps on their knees, expiating their sins and sorrows. In the morning, merchants line the Via Dolorosa, sitting in front of their shops, surrounded by crèches, rosaries and crucifixes. They also sell rough-hewn crosses two meters tall. According to Frieda, the real Via Dolorosa lies buried deep under the debris of wars and sieges. In the afternoons, the shops are closed by order of the

Intifada, shuttered by metal gates scrawled with graffiti. Hate hangs gloomily over the deserted street. The pilgrims have gone on to Tiberias, or to the River Jordan, or over to the Mount of Olives. They're not interested in the people who live here; they're pilgrims in the Holy Land, following in the steps of their Savior.

Seekers from every corner of the earth come together in Jerusalem. Some go away believing they've found something; they hold it carefully in their hands—the words of a rabbi, the aura of a holy place. But hardly have they left the enchanted labyrinth of golden stone than their treasure dissolves. In the daylight of reason, they find themselves with nothing more than what they always had, their vision is a mirage in an Arabian fairy tale.

Irene Wittrich lived in the same neighborhood where my parents had built a house. Wearing a dirndl skirt and a beribboned straw hat, she walked past our garden every Sunday on her way to and from church. To me her piety seemed self-righteous and aggressive. She was a leader of the youth group, and once, after the Procession of Corpus Christi, she tried to recruit me. I said I'd come to meetings when I had less homework but I never went, not even when she invited me to the Carnival celebrations the following winter. I was afraid I would be asked to do something I couldn't do, recite a prayer I didn't know or sing a song I hadn't learned, and people would start to ask questions.

I had been baptized and went to Sunday school, but no one at home talked to me about religion. My grandfather took me to church with him and on holidays I went to the village church with my relatives. My father's sister, whom I stayed with, treated me like an intruder whose presence was based on a presumption of belonging, a spurious bond, easy to expose for the fraud it really was.

"Of course, you don't know that," she'd say, grinning conspiratorially at the others. "Your grandmother never taught you." There were no concrete expectations, nothing that I might have actually learned, only allusions, mean remarks and whispers which I tried to make some sense of. Even the names in my family were a mystery: Aunt Wilma was really Genia, and my grandmother, whom everyone called Beatrice, was actually named Rivka. Though no one ever said anything it seemed to me that I too had stolen my name and had no right to it.

"Edelstein," our German teacher said, walking between rows of desks and up to one of the pupils. "You must be of Jewish descent." This was years after the war but I sensed the threat, and so, apparently did the girl Edelstein. "No, I'm Catholic," she denied the charge. "My grandfather only bought the name."

I stared into my notebook feigning disinterest. My alibi was secure, I was safe, and I had no reason to feel ashamed, and yet I did, as if I had committed treason.

That autumn I went to synagogue for the first time, but not before several failed attempts. First, I made a detour on my way home from school, just to go past the building. Then one Friday I decided to go in, but when I saw the people standing at the entrance, greeting one another like old friends, my courage left me. How did Jews greet one another, did they just say hello? "God be with you" seemed too Catholic. A week later, I walked in, listening very attentively as I made my way to the last row of benches. The women were saying "Happy New Year"; without knowing it, I was observing the Jewish new year for the first time. The congregants shook my hand and smiled with a look of curiosity, but it took years before I overcame my shyness and began to feel as if I belonged. That I was alienated from the community in which I grew up did not mean that I'd automatically be able to slip into the other.

Nurit would understand these thoughts, she loves ambiguities. I've never been able to reveal or explain both sides to anyone: showing one side, I deny the other; then the self I deny attacks the one I choose, accusing my German identity of forcing itself on the Jews for the wrong reasons. My grandmother used to say that turning back to your roots is always possible if you really want it, but the way she lived sent a different message, and that one was stronger. She also said that cowardice is hard to erase. "Don't lie about unimportant things," she said. "When you lie, make sure that it's worth it."

I can't bring myself to tell Nurit that I was christened and brought up Catholic, just as I couldn't tell Sivan. And this afternoon I'll lie again. I won't tell Irene Wittrich that her trips to the River Jordan and the Church of the Holy Sepulcher don't excite me because I'm a Jew.

We ran into each other in the market at Machane Yehuda and I soon regretted agreeing to meet her. But she'd been so happy to see me, an old acquaintance from home, and she seemed so out of place in the Oriental bazaar. I was touched by her familiar accent and her dowdiness roused something in me akin to homesickness. She was wearing a prissy flowered skirt which billowed out over her ample hips and her hair, dyed a frowzy brown, didn't seem to match her light-colored eyes and freckles.

"I come to Jerusalem several times a year," she explained. "For years now I've been guiding groups of pilgrims, but this afternoon I happen to be free." I still remember, back when I was living with my parents, how she lectured in the rectory and showed slides of the Holy Land. She was a few years older than me, and all summer long she wore a T-shirt with the Dome of the Rock emblazoned on it in red and yellow. She still has her buoyant enthusiasm, always a little excited and breathless. Not until she is seated directly across from me at the Quarter Café, obscuring my view of the Dome of the Rock, do I see the wrinkles under her eyes, the double chin and sagging cheeks.

"And how is your father?" she asks.

"Okay, I guess," I say, knowing that she doesn't really care how he is.

"And you live in New York, I hear?"

"Yes, for a few years, I've got a research project."

I suddenly imagine Ya'akov or Eli coming up the steps with a cheerful "*Shalom*, Devorah," and there I'd be, someone else entirely, sitting with Irene Wittrich. I'd have to make a Solomonic choice and to one of them I'd be a liar.

I ask Irene about her life and she answers willingly, talking with growing enthusiasm about how she just can't stay away from the Holy Land, especially Jerusalem, it's become an obsession for her. Many years ago in the Garden of Gethsemane she had her first profound religious experience, she explained.

"This certainty, have you felt it too?" she asks.

"Certainty? No, never in my life," I say.

She is here to follow her calling, which is to protect the peace of the holy sites. She tells me about the masses and processions, the wonders and divine manifestations that happen all the time in this city sacred to the three major religions. That's why

Judgment Day will take place in the City of the Dead in the Valley of Kidron, she is sure, and it will be good to be there when it happens.

"You really believe that?" I ask.

She looks at me, astonished. "If I didn't, would I have made the Holy Land my life's work?"

She believes that the Lord's grace will provide for peace. She talks of Him as a good friend, a powerful bureaucrat whose protection she can count on. I look at her skeptically.

"Well then, you just haven't come that far yet," she concludes patiently. "Some of us find Him later than others."

I do not contradict her. I shake my head and smile—perhaps she finds me arrogant and condescending.

"Some things take time," she insists, "and there are things we can't do alone."

Friends in Tel Aviv had warned me not to stay in Jerusalem too long. The city'll drive you crazy, they said, the place is crawling with lunatics and fanatics. I'm not sure to which of these groups Irene Wittrich belongs, but I suspect the city is beginning to get to me, too. If I were to tell people about my affair with a man who said he was Armenian, they probably wouldn't care. So what? So he lied—why get so excited, why feel guilty and scared?

"You should stay longer and drink in the atmosphere," Irene Wittrich advises me. "Maybe I could help. I'll be in Jerusalem until Friday noon, and then the pilgrims are going up to the Sea of Gennesaret." She pushes her address on me.

I say, yes, thank you, we'll run into each other again, I'm sure, and head down to the Western Wall, certain she won't follow me there.

"We must get together again," she calls after me. "I know you're on the right path!"

In my hotel room, I prepare myself for interrogation.

"Where were your parents during the war?" they'll ask. "Let's start with your father."

"He was with Hitler's Wehrmacht on the Eastern Front."

"Was he a member of the Party?"

"No, he wasn't, but his brother Karl was. Karl was even praised in an article in the *Völkischer Beobachter*. He stormed our city hall with his Storm Troop even before the army marched in and was received with open arms by the jubilant masses."

How do I know that? Not from family records, that's for sure. The story they tell is that Uncle Karl quickly saw the error of his ways and returned from the front a broken man. He was dead before fifty, cirrhosis of the liver. My parents took over his stationery shop when he was in the hospital and visited him every day. No one ever asked him what he'd actually done at the front, they just felt bad for him and his sorry fate. He was only a hanger-on, they said, insignificant, young, easily led. It shouldn't be so hard to understand. But behind his back my Aunt Wilma called him *"Führer"* and would never so much as acknowledge his presence.

"She should shut her trap," Hilde, my father's mother, said. "I could tell a story or two, things so filthy I wouldn't mention them in front of the child."

I had to piece it all together from allusions, archives and birth certificates, from the files of the Third Reich and pages of the *Völkischer Beobachter*. I devoted my entire senior year to it and found a lot of names I recognized. Every afternoon I sat in the library and had brittle old newspapers in marbleized binders brought to my desk, if only to bring a modicum of reality to Martha's portrait. I wanted to get inside her fear and imagine the man who deserted her.

But I failed to uncover a single trace of the woman. The city's wartime history, on the other hand, couldn't have been easier to research—the race laws, evacuations, and deportations were all on record. At the library's checkout desk I heard the name of a high-ranking SS official; when I wheeled around it turned out to be a young woman with overdue books whose family was amply represented in the local phone book. Perhaps she was his grand-daughter or great niece; maybe she'd only married into his family the way my mother had married into Uncle Karl's. She can't be blamed, I thought, she's much too young.

Nevertheless, the more I read, the harder it was for me to retain my fair-mindedness. All over the city, I started to hear names that had popped up in the documents; I could no longer suppress my outrage, even toward myself. I'd look at people and wonder, Where were you then? What did you do? How do you feel about it today? Even my own father kept quiet about the war and I wasn't close enough to him or bold enough to insist on a conversation.

Looking for Martha in municipal records I began to unravel my own mother's family history. My grandmother, Beatrice, had moved from Bohemia to Vienna, where she'd married her hus-band, a reputable lawyer assigned to a post in the provinces shortly after their wedding. His name was also Karl, a good-natured but taciturn man, whose love Beatrice only truly came to know when she saw him suffer humiliation, contempt, and eventually the loss of his government position because of her Jewish ancestry. All this he did without losing his quiet dignity. Beatrice had told me how, as an eight-year-old in Bohemia, she'd taken care of Martha, her aunt's newborn baby, and that it had made her feel very grown-up. Later, when they were both young women, the gap in their ages no longer mattered and Martha was as close to her as a sister. When her mother, my great-grandmother, died, Beatrice was thirteen and her younger brother six years old. Her father remarried, to a Christian woman. Of all Beatrice's family, only Martha did not hold this second marriage against her uncle; the rest of the relatives in Bohemia cut him off, which is why Beatrice never found out what happened to them during the Nazi occupation.

My great-grandmother's name has been erased from the birth certificates and other documentation. The second wife's name and her Aryan family tree has been entered in its place, although she herself was only sixteen when Beatrice, her "daughter," was born, and in fact only married her husband fourteen years later. The records were fixed, making a half-Jew and quarter-Jews of my grandmother and her daughters according to the Nuremberg Laws, diluting the blood just enough to ward off an immediate threat.

I never dared ask Aunt Wilma about "the scandal"—she would have screamed and stormed out of the house and it would've been my fault. "We have to treat her very gently," my grandmother used to say, "she's impulsive and temperamental." My father's sisters called her vulgar, a low-down slut, otherwise she'd never have done *that*. What did she do?

"Well, the man was married, after all," I heard Grandma Hilde say. "A big shot, with a lot to lose. I can't understand why he got involved with her in the first place. What did she think he was going to do for her? It's not like her life was at stake, only her father's job and he lost that anyway."

I only learned the facts behind the scandal years later, after Wilma's death of peritonitis. She'd had an affair with a prominent Nazi, which had enabled her to fix the documents and keep her job. I would have liked to ask her why she was so defensive and ashamed. Until her death she acted the rash, temperamental woman, and although she had become rather heavy she was still beautiful and aristocratic, far more so than my mother. Now, more than ever, I would like to know whether she really loved that man, or whether it was cold will and calculation.

Love and politics—there's always a chance that blood or circumstance will pair you with your enemy, someone you would love with impunity in other times, but to do so now is treason—through no fault of your own. Your secret might be tightly guarded and you might even escape detection but the shame will last your whole life.

Channa-Frieda and I talked about this one afternoon while sitting on her veranda, watching the sun slip into the ravine of Ein Kerem. She asked about my relationship with my mother, who had just died the previous year.

"She was always a stranger to me," I said. "I didn't hate her, I wasn't even indifferent, it's just that I never understood her. She wanted to be loved, she suffered from loneliness, but she always held herself back. I'm sure her inability to communicate made her unhappy but she covered it with an arrogance that seemed like disdain to everyone else. Right up to her death I was never certain whether she really had no warmth or was just inhibited."

"Don't you understand?" Channa said. "She was the child of a mixed marriage. All her life she had to drag her Jewish half around and she probably hated it. Of course, she might have loved it, too, because it distinguished her from everyone else and belonged only to her."

"You may well be right," I said and thought of how my mother always colored her hair blond, even as an old woman. No one was more reserved and dignified. She never laughed out loud or gestured with her hands when she talked. Wilma was just the opposite, but, like her sister, she consigned the past to silence.

Channa listened to me telling Wilma's story as if it were a gossip item I had no right to pick apart.

"There are so many stories," she said, evasively. "Who knows what really happened? You can't make easy judgments about anything that went on then. Stop tormenting yourself—you'll never be able to get to the truth."

Channa dwells in the restful atmosphere of a life which has been well-lived, for the most part. Her composure and clarity keep bringing me back to her in my search for answers. It occurred to me that Martha might look like her, though she'd be over eighty by now. In Vienna, she and Channa had spent a lot of time together. For a few weeks she had even gone out with my great uncle, Rivka-Beatrice's brother, but then he emigrated to Chicago. My grandmother had moved to the provinces with her husband and two daughters, but Martha was still living a tempestuous life in bohemian Vienna. An emancipated woman with no fixed income or enduring relationships, she had moved to Vienna to study philosophy, but then discovered photography. She lived with a painter who married her two years before the *Anschluss* in 1938 and left her immediately after it. That was all Channa knew.

When I was a student in Vienna I met the daughter of Martha's painter. When she told me her name and who her father was I put it together. The chance encounter was astounding, but by then I was so focused in my search for Martha, so obsessed with her, like a detective after his quarry, that I believed the meeting was predetermined. Martha was the motor which gave my life its direction.

The painter's daughter, Gaby, was younger than me, pale and plain, with sleepy blue eyes. She looked like her father but had not inherited his charm. Like a spy, I insinuated myself into her life and family, warily, discreetly, taking care not to arouse suspicion. I told Gaby enough about myself to whet her curiosity. Her parents accepted me with a generosity that sometimes made me feel ashamed. They invited me along on family holidays and I sat among them concealing my feelings with a smile. The aging artist started flirting with me and I wondered what it was about him that had so fascinated Martha. He had a melancholy air, a seductive way of looking at you, and affected a deep appetite for living that was clearly false. Watching them, I learned many things they did not tell me. At the same time, his unsuspecting wife made me her confidante and told me her life story.

Gaby's mother was twenty years younger than Martha, an unreformed Nazi intent on keeping up a respectable appearance yet prone to emotional outbursts. When she and the painter got drunk in the evenings he would talk about his disgust with life while she boasted of her sexual prowess.

I imagined the way he must have been in 1938—ambitious, intoxicated by the new movement, and long since bored with the high-strung woman who was tyrannized by a daily vision of her own destruction. Martha, who wanted to emigrate, had dragged him to the extreme outer edge of his own society when he had always felt thoroughly at home in its complacent center. Martha exposed him to danger. While all Vienna welcomed the new era, deathly fear wormed its way into their lives.

Maybe his family pushed him to get a divorce. Family and friends had also tried to force my grandfather, saying they had his best interests at heart. After all, there was his career to consider, he was young and just starting out. Maybe Martha and the painter might have stood their ground and managed to slog their way through the bad years if that young woman hadn't shown up, the daughter of an influential family and heiress to a company which began to flourish once Jewish competition was eliminated. Her father, a Nazi from the early days, had great influence in the new times.

Gaby's mother first laid eyes on the painter when they were putting up decorations for a Carnival. He was standing on a table and she was handing him garlands. "Right then," she said, "I knew that I wanted him and would get him." In the spring of 1938 he spent several weeks in Vorarlberg and she joined him there. For three days they never left his room or his bed, she bragged. The first time they put in a public appearance at the inn, he casually mentioned that he had a tuxedo ready and waiting in his closet. There was no mention of a wife. Gaby denied that her father had ever been married before.

Martha had fallen through a crack and for many years I could not find a trace of her. Now I can reconstruct her history up to the day she escaped Vienna but there was no return address on her letter from Prague, Channa said, the last letter she received. Who can say Martha didn't survive? Maybe she wanted to start a new life after the war with a new name. I won't give up my search even if it is absurd and it is—for there really is no reason to believe that she's still alive.

The painter married into the right circles and so was saved from going to the front. He fathered a son, who died at age five, and then a daughter. And he kept quiet. He sealed off his past so effectively that even his daughter contended there'd been no first wife. Only once, the mother confided that she'd been so good in bed that she'd even trumped a Jewish woman. When I pressed her she conceded that her husband had been engaged to another woman. I got no more out of her.

Gaby felt guilty, not about her father's betrayal, of which she knew nothing, but about her grandfather, the old Nazi; she owed her affluence to his appropriation of a Jewish firm. Sometimes I envied her unambiguous guilt; her battleground was clearly defined. I incited her to question her parents about things I never dared ask at home. Instead, I spent months in libraries and court archives, wading through stacks of old newspapers and official records. I have my search for Martha to thank for my research skills.

To get beyond silence, on the pretext of research, I signed papers promising not to name names, commit libel, expose collaborators and murderers. I agreed to accept lies and rationalizations. In the District Court's archives, to which I'd been admitted for a few hours, I almost suffocated from the musty decay of old files preserving crimes which can never be redressed. Gaby left the country and I heard that she died before the age of thirty. The painter took his own life. I'll never know whether a portrait of Martha was found among his personal belongings.

$\mathcal{E}$ight years after stumbling across the painter I found Channa in Jerusalem. Back then she was still working and her son lived nearby. I came from Vienna on my first trip with Alvin, just a year after we'd been married.

When I called Channa from the hotel I intended to explain why I'd been trying for years to find her. Instead I blurted out, "My husband left me yesterday."

"Where are you?" she asked, as if she were entirely familiar with the circumstances of my life.

"In the desert, no, now I'm in Jerusalem, but we were in the desert yesterday."

"What happens in the desert doesn't count," she said. "Come right over."

Later, once we'd gotten to know each other, she applauded my direct approach. "I liked that," she said. "It was a cry for help that could not be put off."

What if I'd said my prepared piece: "Do you remember Martha, I've been looking for her for years, maybe you can help me"? I'm not sure Channa would have so readily invited me over for coffee and cake.

"First eat something, it'll calm you down," she started. "It won't seem quite so bad once you've eaten. Things always seem worse before you've had a chance to think them through." I gulped her scalding coffee. "Now, tell me everything."

"You remind me of my grandmother," I said. "She always told me to 'eat first, talk later.' It was supposed to calm the nerves."

The truth is that other than her coffee and cake, she didn't remind me of my grandmother. Beatrice-Rivka would never have lived on her own like this robust woman in her late sixties who made her own decisions. For years, my grandmother never left the house and later she never did it gladly. Her fear of the streets grew with age and began to infect her whole being. She walked, carefully, as if the streets were covered with ice, her movements kept to a minimum, her face set in a sullen mask. She walked like that at home, too. In the end, after years of being overweight and barely moving at all, she could hardly climb the stairs to the third floor.

"So what happened with your husband?" Channa asked. "What were you fighting about?"

"I'm not sure exactly," I said. There were a few words, a truth which had long needed telling, and his final, irrevocable good-bye.

I'd lived a long time without love. Every so often, the absence of love felt like an ailment that would eventually cripple me even though I was happy with my work and friends. But after the first few months of infatuation with Alvin I lost interest. So this is how it is, I thought, there's nothing more to relationships than this.

"Maybe he'll come back," Channa offered consolation. "Maybe it's not so final."

"Yes it is," I insisted.

I stored his image in my mind as he got out of the car we'd rented in Tel Aviv. He was small and scrawny, used up somehow; he seemed like a stranger disappearing into the crowd. I felt no regret, only relief.

"How long were you married?"

"A year."

I could count the good memories on one hand. An extravagant spring in full bloom, in which the lush white and pink blossoms obscured the first green buds on the trees. I remember nothing about our daily life, only the hikes, the afternoon walks, the fruit trees redolent in the evening haze. For months we lived in a state of intoxication in which we didn't quite see each other. And then one day I no longer knew how I could've been infatuated with this man, and what made me think I could spend the rest of my life with him. At first, I thought boredom was a sign of intimacy and that if we worked at love, it would come, in the same way we acquire other skills.

Alvin and I grew up in the same city. We went to the same schools, mixed with the same people, and used the popular catchwords of our generation. We knew each other well. I could guess his thoughts and trace the origin of every shadow, every twinge in his face. I couldn't understand why we were becoming more distant, and what it was that irritated us about each other. One of my friends said that we seemed like good roommates who share the expenses and split the laundry duty. "But there are no sparks between you," she said, "no intimacy, no joy when he comes into the room."

Alvin loved nature and tradition; he would much rather have lived in the country. At first he tried to get me to feel at home in the countryside—it was where he felt most at home—but from one trip to the next I couldn't find the small villages on the map. I immediately forgot the names of the little marketplaces and hamlets he adored and living in such places was unimaginable to me. Children would stop their games as we drove through and women would watch us, shielding their eyes from the sun with their hands. I tried to see the endlessly undulating land through his eyes, to appreciate the broad valleys with their hidden streams flowing between brush-covered banks and the mists rising out of damp hollows. We clambered up to mountain lookouts and Alvin could name all the peaks, which hung like hazy clouds on the horizon.

Our excursions reminded me of the field trips we took in school and the essays that followed in praise of autumn or spring. Once we stopped at an old blacksmith shop and stepped back in time. Alvin and the smithy were sunk in conversation, utterly absorbed in the moment. I watched the eighty-year-old man's wrinkled face in the dusty light filtering through a dirty windowpane and looked at his smooth, shiny head and the mace he held in his hand. Suddenly I saw a forty-year-old man holding an ax and felt fear knocking in my chest. Alvin explained away my terror as hysteria, melodrama, and his lack of understanding drove a wedge between us. Over the course of time it split us in two.

Maybe we'd have gone on for years side by side without understanding what it was that had destroyed our fleeting harmony, had we stayed at home or traveled only to countries equally insignificant to both of us. But I had just gotten hold of Channa's address and had a project to complete—not one that I wished to share with him. So we went to Israel—I as if returning from a long exile with Alvin, a stranger, in tow. I'd come home, but he became more and more alienated each day and we blamed each other for what was happening. Every sentence became a source of misunderstanding and icy silence. For the first time I felt embarrassed at his self-righteous lack of humor and provincial gawkiness, which I had always accepted as a part of him. With Alvin I was a mere tourist; he was furious when I spoke Hebrew and interrupted me in a country German dialect he knew I didn't like.

I had come back to a life in which he had no part, and about which he had not the least knowledge. At the beach in Caesarea I willed him to move away, thinking "Sit over there. Don't hover

over me. I don't want to see you. I want to remember the way it was before you were ever in my life." The beach was where we celebrated Gilbert's twentieth birthday with tubs of hummus, salty pita and sweet Carmel wine from the kibbutz. It was the first time in my life that I'd slept out in the open, and the sparkling sea, the surf, the stars almost drove me crazy. I felt that heaven and earth had been set in motion, but it was only the wind blowing sand in our sleeping bags and the next morning, when the sun beat down on us at six o'clock, it crunched between our teeth. My past separated me from Alvin, though he struggled against it with his irritable presence.

"This is our vacation, forget what happened before, you're with me now."

"You're behaving like an Austrian," I said to him once.

"I am one," he replied tersely, then closed his lips in a firm line.

"Say something, will you? I can't stand this silence," I said. "You're tormenting me with this endless reproach. I want to feel light and be happy. I used to be very happy in this country."

We spent the torrid midday hours in the Jordan Valley in the dense shade of reeds and eucalyptus. Alvin slept leaning against the trunk of a plane tree, his feet dipping in the loamy water. The Jordan River hadn't changed. The willows still trailed their branches in the shallow waters, the brown earth was still damp, the plane trees still shed their bark while their dead branches rustled. Tall, luxuriant tamarinds brushed the shore, birds and cicadas chattered noisily. "Romeo and Juliet!" the kibbutzniks had shouted, hunting for me and Gilbert in the bushes.

"Reminds me of the Danube near Hainburg," Alvin said, as he opened his eyes. "I didn't have to come to Israel for this."

"Joshua never crossed the Danube," I said.

"Well yes, but did Joshua have the right to do it?"

We had found our topic.

"And you say *he* left *you*?" Channa asked.

"He was an anti-Semite," I rationalized.

"An anti-Semite and you married him?"

"Okay, an anti-Zionist, isn't that the same thing? He didn't know any Jews at home but he certainly didn't like the people here."

"He liked you, though," Channa wouldn't let it go.

"In the beginning he was fascinated, I was the first Jew in his life. Then he just got used to me."

"Did you ever tell him your whole story?"

"Do I have to tell everyone every little detail?"

"No, not everyone, but certainly the man you married," Channa said. "Why did you actually split up? What did you fight about?"

"After all his hostility and insinuations," I said, "I told him."

"Told him what?"

"That all you have to do is scratch the surface and there's the anti-Semite."

"You should know," Channa said.

I didn't stay very long after that. We didn't even talk about Martha.

After I rented the car, Sivan and I were no longer stuck in Jerusalem. We could go anywhere.

"Hebron," I said.

"The Dead Sea," Sivan answered.

"But I want to go to the West Bank, I'd like to see Hebron."

"You're nuts, it's dangerous."

"Why are you always playing my protector?"

"You foreigners always think you know better, but you don't have the slightest idea. Whatever I say, you always act as if you knew it already. You never admit that you don't know. The Americans are the dumbest and the Germans are the next dumbest." He grinned at me.

We drove eastward around the Old City wall toward Nablus Street and down into the Judean Desert. Here, in the parched brown desert mounds and dips that unfold like giant sand dunes, in the vast melancholy of isolation and timelessness, I felt that I knew Sivan and he knew me, despite our differences and against all probability.

"My God, it's beautiful," I shouted. Sivan just lit two cigarettes and placed one between my lips. Before we left East Jerusalem he had me stop at the edge of the road and got out to buy water at a kiosk with a low, corrugated iron roof. I sat in the car and watched how he talked with the shopkeeper, at ease, warm and familiar. At first, I wanted to get out with him. "Stay," he said, "I'll be right back, it's not good for you to get out." Why did he keep me hidden? For his sake or mine? Who was endangering whom? He was always nervous in Arab neighborhoods, as if he were doing something forbidden.

"Are you ashamed of me?" I asked, when he returned. He leaned over and kissed me.

Usually it was late afternoon when we drove down into the desert. The sun hung low over the red ridges and the ravines began to fill up with blue shadows. At the last gas station before

Jericho, two soldiers stood at the side of the road thumbing a ride.

"Are you going to pick them up?" Sivan asked.

"I think it's the right thing to do," I said. "After all, they are protecting us."

He didn't answer. I was growing used to his silence.

The soldiers asked Sivan where he lived and he gave them the same story he'd told me, calmly, with no trace of anxiety. But looking on, I could detect a slight stiffening, a tinge of aggression, as if they were interrogating him. He spoke mono-syllabically, cutting off the conversation. Worlds lay between them and him and I was caught in the middle. The soldiers had to be back to training camp by six, and they were late.

"We're not going to make it," one of them said. "It's already half-past five." They were scared, like children late for school.

"We can take you right there," I said, and Sivan turned toward me, horrified, imploring.

We drove deep into the Judean mountains. The colors had dulled but a gentle, forgiving sun still shone on the tents of the army base. After the soldiers took their backpacks out of the trunk, Sivan begged me, "Please, let's go now."

"I want to look around, I've never seen an army camp up close before."

"Just go, dammit, we're making the guards nervous."

"They're not nervous, you are," I said angrily, but I pulled out.

After a few curves in the road Sivan put his hand on my arm and offered me the bottle of water. "Drink," he murmured. "I'm sorry, but they photograph every car that comes up to the camp."

"So what? All we did was bring some soldiers back."

I broke the long silence. "What were they saying? I didn't understand it all," I said.

Sivan was distracted. "What would happen if war broke out right now?"

Once, when it was still light, we drove down to the Dead Sea. We didn't go into the water and sat apart from the bathers. Away from other people Sivan's defiant gloom disappeared and we found our way back to each other.

Far from the beach, where the rocks jut out into the sea, we picked up stones and threw them into the water to see who could throw the farthest. I gave up quickly and just looked on; so much drive and energy for a game, I thought. Watching him, I saw the thrust of his arm and the intent concentration on his face, as if the sea were his adversary, and I was reminded of the images on television and in the newspapers: masked Palestinians throwing stones, young men with the same motion frozen in a pose, the same energy directed at a target that had been cropped out of the picture. Sivan had forgotten me entirely; he was stoning the sea again and again with a ferocity that I'd seen before; it flared up and died down for no clear reason.

"Let's go," I said, chilled. "It's late."

We didn't say a word all the way back up to Jerusalem.

The quickest route took us through a Hasidic neighborhood. We stopped at a junction where two black-hatted, gabardine-clad Hasids were helping an older man across the road, one on each side of him. His arms were slung over their shoulders and his pants hung down around his knees exposing long white underwear.

"Drunk," Sivan said, disgusted.

"Come on," I said. "It looks like he collapsed."

"Why do you think that?"

"Jews don't drink," I said.

He let out a gruff snort. "Drive slowly. They act like there are no cars on the road."

It wasn't easy to make our way through the narrow streets. "It's like they live in another world, in another time," I said.

"They're just crazy." Sivan shrugged. "They live in the twentieth century like the rest of us."

"I don't think you like Jews much," I said.

"I like you," he answered.

My friend Eli, the mystic, was up north in Safed, visiting his family. When I drove there to see him, Sivan accompanied me as far as Jericho, like a considerate husband or brother. I didn't tell him I was going to meet a friend. I was afraid of his jealousy.

That afternoon, the desert lay bleached and boundless under a lemon-colored sky. We followed curve after curve down into the throbbing heat of the Jordan River basin, where the air was like viscous fire. I looked over at Sivan from time to time to see if he was sleeping. When we neared an army checkpoint, Sivan gave a start and sat straight up in his seat, wide awake.

"Stop, don't you see the checkpoint?"

Two battered cars with the blue license plates of West Bank Palestinians were pulled over at the side of the road. Soldiers were bending down looking into the trunks. I kept going.

"Stop," Sivan screamed. "Are you crazy?

"I have an Israeli plate, I never have to stop."

The soldier at the checkpoint waved us through with a tired flick of his hand. Sivan leaned out of the window and yelled something I didn't understand but no one cared, we were already out of earshot.

"Do you see the shutters, the doors boarded up?" he pointed toward Jericho. "Everything closed, you wouldn't believe there used to be nightclubs and bars all the way down this street. I used to come here a couple of times a week."

"When?"

"Before the Intifada. Now it looks like this. No one comes here anymore."

To me Jericho has always looked the same, dusty streets under a brooding sun, small clusters of men standing idly in doorways or sitting under dirty umbrellas advertising Seven-Up. The men looked as if they'd been sitting like that all day long and on into the night, heads bowed and hands hanging between their knees, a glowing cigarette between their fingers, exactly the way Sivan used to sit waiting for me.

Just beyond the last houses of Jericho, he had me stop. "I have to go back," he said and kissed me.

I didn't ask how he was going back. This was his turf.

But he couldn't quite leave, and for a second time he unfolded my map and ran his finger along the road heading north.

"There, up to Beit Shean, then you keep to the right, okay?"

"There's only one road. I won't get lost."

The sun's rays speared the mountain peaks, the desert slopes had begun to turn a pale pink, and we were still parked by the side of the road just beyond Jericho.

"Here's your water." Sivan lined up three bottles. "That should be enough to get you to Tiberias. And cigarettes." He gave me his. Then he cleaned the trash out of the glove compartment and emptied the ashtray. "You should take care of your car.

And now I have to go." He kissed me again as if sealing an under-standing. "I'll see you back in a week, at two-thirty, under the UNRWA sign before the refugee camp."

"So much could happen in the meantime," I said.

"What could happen?" he asked, alarmed.

"You could meet someone. Or I could. I wouldn't start mak-ing any long-term plans."

Sivan shook his head emphatically. "I'm not going to meet anyone. I don't meet people that easily. Maybe you do, but I don't." Then he lit another cigarette. "Let's smoke this before I go," he said, but we kissed instead.

"Don't stop for anyone as long as you're in the West Bank. The gas tank is full. Everything should be okay."

"You take such good care of me," I said.

"Because you're going to come back to me. Don't stop, okay?" he repeated. "Don't pick up any men."

"Except soldiers of course," I threw in.

"No soldier, no matter what!" he yelled. "Soldiers are the worst."

"You can't be serious," I laughed. "You don't think I'm going to leave a soldier standing alone on a road in the West Bank, do you?"

Sivan mulishly repeated what he'd just said. "Soldiers are the worst."

We embraced.

"You have to get going," he said, pointing to the now-purple mountain ridge behind which flames licked the sky. He closed the door, only to open it again, lean across the empty seat, kiss me again, lock the door from the inside, and slam it shut. Right then I wanted to drive back to Jerusalem and spend the night with him.

But I started the car, headed north, and looked back in the wing mirror, watching Sivan get smaller and smaller.

The steep shafts of desert mountain were cowed by the dark violet sky and sadness gathered in the night-blue wadis. Without Sivan, I had nothing to protect me from the desolation of the desert at night. I had left him by the side of the road. He loved me, it seemed. But every time I found myself believing it, I shook the warm thought out of my head. Ridiculous, falling for a child I knew nothing about.

Once I'd passed the moonscape of wadis and craters and was approaching Beit Shean, it occurred to me that the distance might well be saving me from something dangerous, some secret activity of Sivan's. Now the landscape which flashed by was dotted with towns which were obviously Jewish; the flat land with orchards of palm trees and banana plantations belonged to kibbutzim. By the time I parked the car in Tiberias, it was dark. At our meeting point on the boardwalk Eli was there waiting for me.

Later, as we drove into the mountains of Galilee, I told Eli things I thought I couldn't tell anyone. It was surprisingly easy, the story almost told itself. I don't know what suddenly made me open up—maybe it was because I saw how out of place Eli seemed, standing there on the boardwalk in his embroidered yarmulke and bright-colored caftan, and I felt comfortable with his otherness.

Below us, smaller and more distant with each upward curve, lights flickered around the sea, outlining its contours; above us there was nothing but vast open space and a moon like a crushed orange. And I talked because it was as easy as floating up out of the depths to the water's surface.

"You're wrong if you think we've got so much in common because we love this country and share the same religion. You feel an inalienable right of ownership that has always escaped me. I hover at the edge, expecting to be driven out if it looks like I'm getting too comfortable. I'm convinced that I've snuck into this place, any place, and that it's painted all over my face. I'm always an illegal alien. And you know what? Even if they let me stay, I'm sure it's just on trial, until they find out who I really am. Years ago I actually believed I was some kind of peacemaker and it was my mission to reconcile the two sides, but too much has happened for that."

"So you come from a mixed marriage?" Eli asked.

"Worse, half my family is ashamed of its Jewishness and feels guilty about having denied it. The other half . . . It was years before I really knew anything about my family, and I was constantly exposed to accusations from my father's relatives. For a while I tried to make myself fit, until I found out that they're the ones who are guilty."

"Wasn't the decision made for you? I thought you were born Jewish," Eli said.

"If only it was that simple. I grew up Catholic and didn't know my grandmother was Jewish. I did know that a Jewish background was something you were supposed to hide. A person wants to be proud of their family but me, whichever way I turned, there was always the other side—if I said I was Jewish then the Catholic part got offended; if I tried to defend the Catholic half then the Jewish part felt betrayed. And if I tried to plead extenuating circumstances for one side, then the other writhed in pain."

Eli didn't understand. "There's always a line between right and wrong, victim and perpetrator."

"But what if you have a share in both? It's demoralizing to be both victim and perpetrator. Guilt-ridden self pity—try putting that in the bank. If I identify with the victim then I suspect myself of trying to avoid responsibility. It drives me crazy."

"Look," Eli said, "you only have to answer for yourself, you don't need the group's seal of approval to know who you are."

"That's true if you can choose sides anytime you want and everyone else just accepts your choice. But what if the very freedom to choose disqualifies your choice anyway? When you try as hard as I do to belong, it's just because you're a coward and can't be true to yourself."

"You're losing me. Can't you give me some concrete details?" Eli broke in.

It was the first time I laid out the facts of my life for someone else: My grandmother came from an assimilated Jewish family in Bohemia. She first celebrated Christmas in the house of her Catholic stepmother, and then continued doing so at home with her husband and children. She managed to hold onto some fragments of her Jewish heritage, a few songs, a little superstition and some taboos she didn't understand. She didn't eat pork because of trichinosis, she said, and no shellfish because they eat filth. Bloody food in any form was quickly disposed of. Sometimes she'd throw out one raw egg after the other, down the kitchen sink, because of a tiny red spot in the yolk, frugal though she was. She was suspicious of strangers, but absurdly accommodating. I hated watching the way she'd become subservient and resentful at the same time. It was humiliating. Every time something bad happened she blamed herself for bringing misfortune down upon us all. But in some way she was a living reproach, because she always suffered more than the rest of us. When I began to understand my grandparents' silent marriage, I suspected that she never forgave her husband for his magnanimity in standing by her.

"I loved her, but sometimes I despised her a little, too, and that hurt me. I wish there'd been at least one small rebellion, that she'd done just one outrageous thing to assert herself."

Eli stopped me. "Everyone has a story and it gets told over and over again until it turns into an adventure or a myth. Or they keep quiet until the story is thoroughly repressed. Then the story grows into something monstrous and keeps pushing the poor person up against a wall until he's not much more than his silence. And everyone who's suffered believes that his own story is unique, and forgets that he's a lot like other people."

The sharp curves of Rosh Pina were already behind us and the first of the row houses of the new settlements near Safed began to appear along the road. I didn't know whether Eli had understood me or whether some experiences defied retelling. And I couldn't escape the suspicion that there was something I was trying to evade, that I was holding back in spite of myself. Something was hiding inside, something unfathomable and inaccessible, even to me. There is a dark pit. I stand before it and throw my questions into its depths but, like a landslide, the ground beneath me gives way and the pit sucks me down.

From time to time, traces of people's buried stories surface in old ritual objects, candlesticks, and Kiddish cups for sale at flea markets. They had been stolen from their original owners, and the sons and daughters who inherited these spoils didn't know what to do with them, so they're on display in the open air along with the leather coats and medals that were also no longer of use.

"Why did you choose to be Jewish?" Eli asked, as he searched for a parking place in the narrow, crooked streets.

"It was a restitution that my grandmother couldn't make. And I experienced the return as familiar in a way that I never really understood, as if I was part of a collective memory or something. But being Jewish is not unequivocally mine in the same way that it is yours. It's kind of on leasehold and can be withdrawn, unilaterally, on grounds of bad behavior. Maybe I'd feel differently if I had children."

The moon hung low over the whitewashed walls of Safed; they glowed like sheets, casting angular black shadows. We were quiet and no sound came from the house behind the blue iron gate, only the mulberry trees rustled in the yard, their branches brushing gently against the window panes. Eli carried in my bags and embraced me at the door to my room.

"I'll have to start taking better care of you. As it says in the Song of Songs: 'Why should you wander in sadness among the herds of your friends?' "

Time dragged in the Galilee; it was a long week. I spent much of it yearning for the boy I'd left back in the West Bank.

I like it here, I told myself, but know the area by heart, every stony hill where the coarse, scorched grass reflects the sun's glow. Gilbert and I had hitchhiked on the roads many times and often we'd had to walk in the heat of the day on the burning asphalt, the chirping of cicadas the only sound. The sun drove us crazy. We fought and cried and left one another a dozen times but each evening, after our shower, we'd sit combing each other's hair on the steps of a kibbutz guest house. Later we'd go out to the fields and the orchards to look at the stars. We knew nothing could really separate us, ever. Now, twenty years later, I was traveling the roads in my rented car, happy to see anyone who looked like they needed a ride.

From time to time, when I found some shade, I'd stop the car and lie down among the thistles and rocks and watch the heat shimmering over the Jezreel Valley. I sat at cafés by the water, staring out at the glinting waves until the sun cooled, as if I were waiting for a ship. The hours of driving around could not still the hunger in my heart, nor could the casual conversations I struck up with strangers. I craved a life that would wash away my old self like the breakers that hit the ramparts of Acre Fortress, from which I contemplated the sea. I wanted to be Devorah, a woman with no traceable past. I wanted to cast off the weight that tied me down.

I hardly saw Eli that week. There was always somewhere he had to go and do his healing, his laying-on of hands. His mother tried to entertain me with spicy oriental sauces and stories about her heart disease but I was restless, impatient for Jerusalem. This was an experience I knew well: I'd run from the city and twist myself in circles to get away, but then Jerusalem wouldn't let go. I find no peace until I'm climbing the road that leads me there.

At the end of the week, on the way back, I picked up a young couple from East Berlin. They were sweltering by the roadside, exhausted and burnt red from the sun. It was their first trip to Israel. They were curious and asked a lot of questions about Jewish holidays and traditions. They claimed to know a lot about Israel, but they had only spoken to Palestinians. As for Israelis, they were cold and calculating, rude and unfriendly; they picked up hitchhiking soldiers while backpacking tourists were left standing in the road. The couple would be glad to go home.

"I can take you as far as Jericho," I said, "I wouldn't want you to faint from heatstroke." And that was my last comment for the rest of the drive. The tourists' self-righteous indignation brought to mind my last days with Alvin.

We too had been driving toward Jericho from the north, both anticipating the moment of our breakup. During the previous few days we had become enemies; every sentence that we threw into the silence in a last, timid attempt at understanding served only to widen the breach.

"I just can't stand these people," he said. "They're cold, arrogant and pushy, and you always have to keep an eye on them."

"Which people? Do you mean Jews?"

At that moment I realized he never let the word "Jew" pass his lips. At home he'd say "Jewish," but in Israel it was different—he didn't have to protect "these people" from anti-Semitism; on the contrary, if anyone was in need of protection, it was him. He suspected a rip-off with every purchase, and if he wasn't making a fuss over shekels, it was *agorot*, pennies. His insistence on calculating the exact rate of exchange confused every transaction.

"You never know where you stand with them," he lectured me. "They're manipulative, rational, have no feelings. You're the same way," he said. What he found lacking was heart. "As far as temperament goes, I feel closer to the Arabs," he said.

He watched me suspiciously and kept checking my reactions. Whose side was I on? Every Hebrew sentence I spoke was a betrayal, every smile aimed elsewhere triggered his anger. "Why do you kiss their ass?" he said. "The way you flirt with the men is disgusting."

He kept comparing Israel to Austria. He felt the need to defend his homeland, which clearly was not mine. "You'll keep coming back here," he said, "and then one day you'll stay."

"That would be wonderful," I answered. Our split was all but explicit.

In Beit Shean he parked the car up against a broken down wall. It was all that remained of an old house; the whole area was one big heap of rubble dotted with new houses.

"Look at what they've done," Alvin said. "They've bulldozed whole neighborhoods, flattened everything, pure carnage, as if there was no one here before them. And all these archaeological excavations, trying to prove that they've always been here. Even they know better than that."

When we bought a cold drink Alvin spoke to the old man at the kiosk, who answered him in Yiddish. He had planted trees here, he had built this country, he said. "We've accomplished a lot but there's still more to do." His family had gone up in smoke, through the chimneys, the man said when we asked where he came from. He had married again but there were no children. I was ashamed when Alvin bowed his head and grimaced, showing a sorrow he didn't feel.

"That's the other side of the story," I told Alvin.

"There is no other side, wrong is wrong." He was merciless. We were back on our favorite topic—we just couldn't get away from it. Alvin seemed to need the injustice the Jews had committed against the Palestinians as a kind of leveling stick.

Alvin had told me about his parents soon after we'd met. He hated his father, a minor Nazi official who'd beaten and humiliated him after returning from a post-war detention camp for Nazi functionaries, an intruder into the life of his ten-year-old son. Alvin spoke of his hatred, but his voice was filled with a boy's unrequited love and the pain of early loss. His father's history had cast Alvin with the felons and he was thus condemned to hate him. Alvin could never permit himself to love his father nor understand him.

Israel's wrongdoing seemed to free him from feelings of guilt. By making common cause with its victims, Alvin could see himself as victim, feeling all the more courageous since he was willing to be unfairly labeled an anti-Semite for the sake of justice. And he cast me with the oppressors, with the Israelis. He ticked off on his fingers the razed Arab villages and bitterly accused me of expropriating their land. Sputtering with rage, he pointed out the new white fortress towns on the West Bank, built up for Jewish settlers.

"Look, just look at that. It's a crime, a crime against humanity. There's no justification." He wanted me to admit that Israel was racist, Fascist. Nothing less would do.

We were enemies. Perhaps we had always been enemies and I'd only just begun to notice. But maybe, for the first time, he was allowing himself to hate without feeling ashamed. He couldn't bear my affection for a country he loathed. He hated everything—the heat, the shops, the waiters, the drivers, and he raced through the countryside like a madman, refusing to pick up soldiers or kibbutzniks on their way home. The night before we drove to Jericho, we picked up two young soldiers on the Syrian border. They were waiting on a desolate road marked by empty Arab villages, burnt-out tanks, and deserted army posts. The few buildings were pockmarked with bullet holes. The soldiers sat in the back and we observed each other in the rear-view mirror.

"Where are you from?" I asked.

"Samaria," the younger one answered.

"The occupied territories, you mean," Alvin said, with a sneer.

"No, the liberated territories," the other soldier injected.

"Leave them alone," I pleaded. "Don't you want to hear what they think?"

Alvin stopped the car and made them both get out, in the middle of nowhere, in the dead of night. His inarticulate anger and this act of violence scared me.

"You have no right to take any position," I said. "Just think of your background."

We spoke no more, but there was concentrated hate in Alvin's eyes and in his jerky movements.

Further south, as we jumped over the trenches marking the Jordanian border, Alvin gave me a shell casing as a gesture of reconciliation, but our cease-fire ended in Jericho.

We were both trying hard. With excruciating care, as if every word or touch could wound, we passed food to each other and weighed each sentence as if we were strangers who'd just met. Out of sheer caution we misinterpreted each other and seemed to seize always on the wrong words.

In Jericho we sat on a graffiti-covered wall, exhausted from the drive through the West Bank. Teenagers cycled back and forth, circling around us, not being unfriendly, only wary, until a man came and chased them away. He invited us to his house in the refugee camp, one unpainted room, divided by a curtain. The room was concrete, the walls, the floor, and the ceiling, and we all sat at his bedside, as if we were visiting someone in the hospital. His young wife leaned back on the bed, not ill, there simply wasn't any other place for her to sit. Her eyes followed him, timid and sad, obeying every command. Her first child had died just a few weeks before, perhaps on this bed, too. She smiled gently and pushed wedding pictures into our hand. Then she told us all about her family. Slowly, the room filled with young women and children offering us tea and sunflower seeds.

"One and a half million Palestinians are waiting in Jordan for a visa," the man said, and introduced himself as Walid.

"But that's more than the entire population of the West Bank," I said.

He ignored my challenge. "Are you Jewish?" he asked Alvin. "I couldn't welcome a Jew in my house."

Alvin cast an imploring look my way.

Then Walid dug out his photos too, young men in Western dress with *keffiyehs* on their heads. "Everyone in jail," he said.

"What did they do?" I said.

He refused to acknowledge me and kept filling his tea glass with brandy until the bottle was empty.

"The Jews are giving us problems. This one here," he pointed to one of the young men in the picture, "he used to play soccer and now he's sitting in a wheelchair."

"Electric shock," Alvin spat out bitterly. I detected no sympathy for the man, only anger for the perpetrator.

"What makes you think that?" I asked.

"They tortured him."

"He must have done something," I protested.

"They locked me up, too," Walid said. "You're smart, you're dangerous, you come along, that's all."

"Just like that? No reason?"

He looked at me warily. "You sure you're not Jewish?" he asked Alvin. "They used napalm against the women and children," he went on.

"That's a lie!" I exclaimed.

"They started four wars against us, they attacked us and our leaders betrayed us, just gave them our land, handed over Arab land without even putting up a fight. They're racists and terrorists. They locked up my friends and tortured them!"

"Some of it is probably true," Alvin said.

"Let's go," I said.

On the way to the car Walid pointed a water hose at me. The hard, icy jet hit me in the shins and I screamed. "Holy water!" he shouted, a threat in his eyes. "Jesus bathed here, cross yourself!"

The alleyways were like a little Venice with water canals flowing between the houses. Children leaped over them and ignored us. I felt neither suspicion nor hostility—whoever came that far had a good reason, tourists usually didn't, only sympathizers.

We drove through tiny streets of palms, brick houses, pomegranate trees, and bougainvillea, stopping in an avocado grove behind a cottage and next to a herd of goats to eat the food we had brought—pita bread, feta cheese, and tomatoes. We had no language for what was happening to us, only treacherous words. We were helpless before the distance growing between us. It had been a long time since we looked into each other's eyes.

A young girl came out of the house and brought us a bottle of cold lemonade. She was a student preparing for exams, she said, but the occupation forces had shut down the university.

She and Alvin talked as if I weren't there—they were provocatively close. I couldn't remember ever having heard the soft, sympathetic voice he was using. Before we left, I went to the toilet in the house and when I came back they were still talking, inhabiting a private space for two.

We continued down to the Dead Sea, reaching Ein Gedi by nightfall. It was our last night together and we both lay awake, hoping for a touch, a word, to lead us out of our dead end. In the morning Alvin laid a heavy hand on my shoulder and said that it would probably be better if we each went our own way.

I drove into Jericho in the blazing heat. Sivan was sitting by the roadside in the dusty shade of a crooked old olive tree, not far from the UNRWA sign. He held his crouching posture, as if he'd been sitting there for hours and could continue to do so forever.

"The taxi didn't want to bring me all the way out here," was his reproachful greeting.

"How are you?" I asked him in Hebrew.

"Who are those two in the back?" he answered irritably.

"German tourists. They're getting out at the Dead Sea junction."

"I missed you," I said once we were alone. "There wasn't a single day that I didn't miss you."

"I missed you, too."

"Let's stay in the desert for a while," I said.

We crossed the salt-encrusted moonscape. There wasn't a leaf of shade between Jericho and Ein Gedi, the heat bit into anything that moved.

When we returned to the junction the two backpackers were still waiting.

"Stop," Sivan said. "You can't just leave them here. You said they're East Germans—they probably don't have any money."

"I've had enough of bleeding heart Germans for a lifetime. You know, I was married to one once."

He looked at me with a question in his eyes.

"They have nothing good to say about Israel, they're full of their self-righteous opinions, but they've got no idea what's really going on here. If they don't like Jews let them take their holidays somewhere else."

Sivan said nothing and his resolute silence provoked me into a tirade. I ranted and still he stayed mute. I got tangled up defending Israel against accusations he never made. I railed against his stubborn refusal to respond, hoping for a word, a gesture of agreement. But his face was set, fixed on the road ahead. "Jews are ethical people," I concluded, and for a brief moment I felt his thoughts move next to me like a dark heavy object, a densely compressed mass of resentment and dissent.

"What now?" I said eventually.

"We'll get something to eat. There's a restaurant at the next bend. Stop."

"Why? There's another fifty meters, at least."

"Just stop, okay, and stay in the car. Would you like a falafel?" Sivan got out and then ran back to ask if I'd prefer tahini or hummus?

This relationship is going nowhere, I thought, and watched Sivan bring back Coke and two falafel-filled pitas. He had his mischievous grin that always made his face look even younger. I wondered how many times I'd hurt him, and remembered talking about a friend of mine who wanted to expel all the Palestinians into Jordan. At least Sivan showed me a little more sensitivity than that.

"Shall we go?" he said, holding out a pita.

"What about eating?"

"Later, after we get past the houses."

"I'm sick and tired of playing hide-and-seek."

"Drive carefully," was Sivan's response. "You're not a very good driver. I had a dream," he went on. "I died in an accident. It was your car." Sivan took his dreams very seriously.

"I killed you?" I laughed.

"No, actually I was at the wheel and suddenly the road just vanished. We were in the desert and drove right into a deep wadi, but the brakes weren't working. You were next to me."

I'd begun to anticipate Sivan's changes of mood—they would course through my body as if I were an antenna picking up his wavelength. This had never happened before, this invasion of myself by another person's feelings. Sivan was inside me; he flowed through my limbs, my gut, my joints. I was unarmed, no longer resisting the fear that flooded me periodically like a narcotic wave. I let the fear in without trying to decipher its meaning.

The car hugged a narrow desert track as we drove toward a sheer mountain wall. Villages of mud-colored houses lay beyond the dunes. I guessed at the seam between road and desert and pulled over.

"Let's rest for a moment," I whispered. "It's so quiet. Can you hear the earth holding its breath?"

Sivan curled up in his seat and laid his head in my lap. I looked down at his profile, which seemed to communicate a message I could not decipher. Over the course of the summer the back of his neck had been burned almost black by the sun and his coarse hair scratched my bare legs. I felt anxious and tender in the clear knowledge that I would leave him soon, him and the violet mountains with their sharp silhouettes cutting the turquoise sky. Sivan was part of this landscape while I was only a guest.

By the last rays of twilight we rejoined the road and a rock scraped the bottom of the car, firmly wedging itself in. Sivan crawled under the car. When he got back in he pointed reproachfully to a deep cut in the palm of his hand.

"I'm sorry," I said quietly. "I guess I really am a bad driver."

"Don't worry," he said. "It gets dark so quickly out here, it's not your fault."

As we approached Jerusalem we turned off onto a little-used road leading to a village. We had parked here before, hiding between the tall dunes. "I've been waiting for you all week," I said. "Each day was an eternity between morning and night."

I drew him to me. I had never been so near to a man, at one with his liquid body and beyond my own. I had left my flesh behind, so far behind that every glimmering star over the boundless desert was mine to hold, to pluck out of the heavens and offer my beloved. And then, without warning, my long rapture was pricked by a cold sensation of horror, not strong enough to beat back the joy, but powerful enough to bring me back to the uncomfortable plastic car seats.

The whole car began to rock at the side of the road as if a large animal had swung the car onto its back and was trying to carry it away.

"What is it?" I whispered. "Go take a look."

Sivan slowly got dressed and stayed where he was.

"All right, I'll go," I said.

The wind pressed me up against the car and I choked on my own hair. It scoured the surface of the sand with a high whistle.

The car stood small and motionless between the expanse of sky and the black dunes. Nothing moved. When I try to work out what happened, I feel light-headed. I can't help but ask whether he planned what came next. Could he really have been so cold and soulless? Am I deluded, afflicted with the famous Jerusalem Syndrome which, in my case, has taken the form of a persecution complex? Since Sivan disappeared I haven't been able to shake this madness.

We continued the drive up to Jerusalem and on the way the brakes failed. Drenched in perspiration, I made my way into the city with the emergency brake on.

"I'll have to take the car in tomorrow. God knows what it'll cost."

"My friend could do it," he said. "He'd repair the brakes in a day. Look, I can try and find him right now."

We stopped outside the Lion's Gate. The Old City loomed over us like a hulking fortress. Sivan kept me waiting a long time, and I had some difficulty holding my spot. Buses and cars with West Bank license plates boxed me in and honked angrily. Men wearing long *djellabas* pressed their noses flat up against my window. What in the world was a car with Israeli plates doing in East Jerusalem in the middle of the night? I locked the doors expecting a lit match in my gas tank at any moment. Everyone had heard about Israeli cars suddenly turned into funeral pyres. It happened in broad daylight and here I was with my bare arms and legs alone in the black night.

After an hour or more, Sivan came back. He couldn't find his friend but he'd track him down in the morning.

"I'll be in Gaza all day tomorrow, but I'll be back at around five. Then I'll bring him over to your hotel."

"How are you going to get in touch with your friend if you're in Gaza all day?"

"Don't worry. I'll manage."

"You've got this whole life going on and I never hear a thing about it. Why don't you tell me anything?"

"Because I can't."

But I still trusted him.

I decided to confide in Eli. He had some inkling of what had been going on so I might just as well tell him the rest. On the phone his wife said that he was at the university library on Mount Scopus. It had been twenty years since I was last up there.

Gilbert and I used to spend weekends in the dormitory. We knew a student who went home every weekend and gave us her room. We'd catch the last bus on Friday evening and reach Mount Scopus just in time to see Al Aqsa Mosque burst into light in the flames of the sunset. The cypresses were as black as their oversized shadows and, back then, you could still hear the jackals howl as they came out to woo the desert night. But progress has left few of my memories intact. The hills below the university are no longer wild, the white boulders and gorse have gone along with the grazing goats and the odd stone house. A Hyatt Hotel hugs the slope, terraced in limestone to fit in with the landscape. I could have sworn that the city was closer and the valley wasn't so narrow. Even the distances seem to have changed.

On Sabbath mornings we used to run down Mount Scopus straight to the Old City. By the Lion's Gate a street musician plucked at a bouzouki-like instrument. With only three strings he managed to weave a web of enchantment that ensnared pass-ersby—they'd forget what they were doing, and stand by the hour as if touched by magic. That too could be a trick of my unreliable memory.

Eli was amazed to see me. "You still here?"

"I need your advice," I said.

"Weren't you supposed to leave a week ago?"

I had no idea where to start or how to adjust the story for public consumption. For all I knew, the whole thing was already spread over people's desks or filed away with photos and taped phone calls. They can take pictures at night now, too, with zoom lenses. Maybe they'd even followed me to Mount Scopus. I was putting everyone in danger, Eli, Nurit, Channa, Ya'akov, dragging them down with me. I was contagious, like a disease.

I looked into Eli's smooth, round face and worried eyes. I could still go, I hadn't said a word. No one knew anything for certain and maybe in time my indiscretion would just disappear as though it had never happened. As long as I said nothing.

"If I try to leave I'm afraid the security forces will stop me."

Eli didn't miss a beat. "Let's go for a walk," he said.

"Do you think we might be followed?"

"No," he laughed. "Why in the world would you think that? Boy, Jerusalem really does drive people crazy."

We walked past the law school to the old amphitheater with its stunning view over the desert and down to the Dead Sea. It struck me that Eli had gotten heavier over the past few years and maybe he was wearing the caftan to hide his belly.

"Two months ago, I met an Armenian," I said. "He was kind, attractive, interesting. There was no reason not to be friends. I saw him now and then, he showed me around the city, helped me rent the car. And I met him in Jericho on the way back from visiting you that time."

"A nice young man, eh? Did you sleep with him?"

"Yes."

"I thought so. What is it you say in New York? No free lunch?"

I met him, I liked him, I slept with him. That was the whole story, not so interesting after all. Except for the last bit, which I still can't fathom even after sleepless nights, theories and suspicions, throwing out my theories, and the pointless replay of every little detail. And then I can't quite remember—did that really happen or am I imagining it? Did he say it quite like that? So I start all over again, playing both prosecution and defense. I hold up vague inklings and half-sentences for examination; I scrutinize small moments barely noticed at the time, turning them over for traces of significance that I might have missed.

"So that's it?" Eli broke the silence.

"The day before I was supposed to take the car back I drove over a rock and then the brakes failed. It's the kind of damage the insurance doesn't cover."

"And he helped you with that, too."

"He had a friend, a mechanic. But his friend lived in Ramallah and he had to take the car there to fix it."

"So you went and were frightened and thought now it's going to happen, all those terrible things everyone warned you about."

"Yes, I was frightened."

"Devorah, they're not monsters, you know. I live with them, I have good friends in the West Bank whom I really like and respect."

"But you can't trust them, you said so yourself."

"I don't believe we can put our trust in them as a nation, that's what I said. But as for individuals and hospitality, generosity, living as neighbors, that's something else."

"In Ramallah they took the car and disappeared for hours. I thought I'd never see it again. When they came back we went into someone's house. I didn't understand what they were saying, there was something about my passport. Then we all piled into the car and drove back to Jerusalem. His friend, the mechanic, took the wheel, he said it'd be safer because of the Israeli license plates. He said the car might get stoned otherwise. By now there were five of us in the car and I don't know how fast we were going. A few miles out of Ramallah we came to an army checkpoint. The soldiers shone a spotlight in the window and signaled us to stop but the mechanic turned off all the lights and drove around the roadblock like a madman. We must've been doing at least eighty-five on an unpaved road. We tore into a village with the headlights off and zigzagged through the streets, right out of a chase scene on television. Then the driver pulled over, put me behind the wheel, and pointed me toward Jerusalem. No one stopped us again. They said they'd run the barrier because none of them had a driver's license."

"I don't believe it," Eli said. "You don't risk your life over a driver's license. Do you know what the army does to them if they get caught?"

"So what is it? Something really bad?"

"God, Devorah. I never thought you were such an idiot." Eli was furious. "This isn't Texas, we're at war here, for God's sake. What did you think you were doing on the West Bank in the middle of the night? Whatever made you give him your car key? You're like a baby."

"What should I do?" I asked in a small voice.

"Well, you're lucky he turned off the headlights. They probably didn't get the license number otherwise you'd have heard from the Shin Bet a long time ago. And you know what that means? No sleep, interrogation, and buckets of cold water, at the very least."

"But what were they doing? What happened?"

"To you? Hormones."

"Come on, why did they run the roadblock? What did they want from me in Ramallah?"

Eli sighed. "The car, probably. With Israeli plates they thought they wouldn't get stopped. They could've been smuggling weapons or leaflets. Maybe one of them has gone underground and they needed him in Jerusalem. How should I know? Whatever it was, they had something to hide, something worth risking their lives for. And yours."

We went back to the library. Eli was still angry, as if I'd betrayed him.

"Why don't you go somewhere else, where you can't do so much damage, to Tel Aviv or back up north to visit my mother? Do you have any idea what might've happened?" Eli's rage got a second wind. "They're probably terrorists and your life doesn't mean a thing to them. And who knows? Maybe you've actually done some real harm. Maybe we'll read about it in the papers."

"Eli, what should I do?"

"You should've asked me before. Just stay out of their way, and that goes for your Armenian, too, who probably isn't one. The next time you're looking for adventure could you stick to West Jerusalem?"

We said good-bye at the bus stop. "Keep in touc "Someone's got to take care of you, if you can't do it y

I looked at my watch. It had taken just an hour to tell my story, less than an hour, but I wasn't done with it. Now that I'd started, I wanted to tell it over and over again. First of all, I wasn't crazy. I didn't imagine Sivan's furtiveness and secrecy—I had good reason to be suspicious. It was a relief to find that out, to be back on firm ground. Now I knew that Sivan had used me. When we were together he was thinking of his mission, his objective: me. No wonder I had no clear memory of our conversations; he was on guard with every word he spoke. In his smooth, secretive way, he always had something of the spy about him. Now that I finally knew, everything fell into place. At some point I'd begun to sense it, but I closed my eyes, I was in too deep. Suppose he was a terrorist—that didn't make him incapable of falling in love, feeling affection, giving warmth, and sometimes even forgetting himself and his principles like anyone else.

I needed to leave Jerusalem. After talking to Eli it was clear—I had the information I needed; there was nothing to keep me here. I still wanted to say good-bye to Nurit, Anahita, and Channa. Then I would drive away, probably forever.

The city had slammed its doors on me. I sat in the bus and looked out the window with a bad conscience. I had no business being here. The tall limestone walls hid secluded courtyards from my sight. The trees were gray, the shutters on the houses closed, and the windows of the apartment buildings dark and blind. I had fallen from innocence, although my crime was committed some time ago. The bomb that rips apart a crowded city bus might well have been planted with my help; every terror victim could point his finger at me. I had forfeited my right to be in Jerusalem.

Near the central bus station I sat in a gloomy café filling up on coffee and cigarettes, trying to drive out the misery in my head. Is it a crime to fall in love? I looked beseechingly into the face of the man behind the bar. He grinned back at me.

I had managed to get the rented car back on time, the day after the incident in Ramallah. Sivan came with me right into the office. Doesn't that say something for him? The receptionist took the key, went across the street and drove the car away. I expected a bomb to explode right there, blowing both car and driver to bits. "You'd have heard about it," Eli said. Then Sivan and I went to Tel Aviv for the evening and back to Jerusalem. I, too, went underground. It wasn't planned, and I didn't even notice it at first. Sivan stayed with me for two more days, but he was restless and insisted on moving from one hotel room to another. Then he simply vanished, but I continued flitting about the city, never spending more than a few nights at one hotel before shifting to the next. During the day I wandered the streets, an easy target for anyone who might've been looking for me.

Since then, on many sleepless nights, I've accompanied that car back and forth across the city and watched it explode over and over. In the morning, by the light of day, it seems fantastic, impossible. After all, I tell my exhausted self, Jerusalem is not a jungle.

But still, just in case, I put on my sunglasses before leaving the room and see an assassin reflected in the mirror. But then doesn't everyone have something to hide? Hasn't everyone heard the ping of that decisive moment when they chose to keep silent and let themselves be carried along with events? Don't we all have something of which we're ashamed?

*O*ne summer I took a job with a family in Pennsylvania. The mother, a Bavarian who'd emigrated after the war, wanted a German-speaking au pair for her three American children. "German émigré family" was how she'd described them—exactly what I was looking for. My grandmother's brother had emigrated to the United States during the Depression and maybe Martha herself had ended up in America.

The Bavarian war bride was tall, self-assured, and completely Americanized. She said she'd been living in Pennsylvania "for an eternity" and had left Germany "a long time ago." Her chief preoccupation was domestic order, but I had an easy time there with few responsibilities and many free hours. She asked me to knock on the door before I entered a room and to use each room for its proper purpose—the bedroom for sleeping, the kitchen for cooking, the dining room for eating, and the living room for watching television and receiving guests.

One afternoon I forgot to knock on the living room door and was by the fireplace before she could close her walnut cabinet. Horrified, I saw her secret: a shrine of photographs, an SS uniform and insignia, medals, a smooth face. She fumbled with the little cabinet lock and stood before me as if she expected to be arrested. The briefest of moments, and all her efforts wasted; her painstaking construction of an identity, put together piece by piece, built with lies, allusions, and opinions designed to show her in the most sympathetic light, all cemented with hard-won accent-free English to banish the shame forever—the entire edifice of her postwar self toppled in less than a second. She knew that no explanation, no rationalization, could wipe out what I had seen. From then on we were accomplices guarding her dreadful secret. We were polite but shy. Too embarrassed, we no longer looked each other in the eye. I had lifted the cloth and glimpsed her unspeakable truth.

I found myself heading back to the Old City. Even when I ignore it, turn my back on it, the city wall is the true north of my inner compass. In prayer, my grandmother's family, my family, turned toward Jerusalem three times a day. And for me, too, not a week passes without that involuntary homage. Reading the newspaper my eyes slide eastward, across the Mediterranean, as I check the temperature in Jerusalem. When I look at a clock, I adjust the time forward, seven or eight hours, depending on the time of year. "It's getting cooler," Channa writes in autumn, "I'm wait-ing for the first rain." "Here in New York a cold, raw wind is whipping in off the ocean," I write back. On milky blue winter days, when the air hardens into frost, I think of the clammy damp and the downpours of Jerusalem winters. Like a devout pilgrim, I turn east.

In Bezalel Street I bought a farewell bouquet for Anahita. She could put the flowers with her geraniums and transport herself on their heady scent. "I'm very romantic," she'd confessed to me. "Nobody seems to notice, they think I'm very practical," she said. Only because her dreams have never been fulfilled.

I worried about visiting Anahita, afraid that someone would be waiting for me at the Jaffa Gate. Pierced by the looks of strangers, I kept my glance on the paving stones as if I were counting them. Out of the corner of my eye I thought I saw Ihab, the red-haired merchant from Hebron. He hadn't spoken to me after that one time in his store, but he certainly saw me. He stood in the door of a tea shop talking to someone and nothing escapes him. I was grateful for the impersonal, guileless looks of a group of tourists huddled in the shade around the entrance to David's Tower, waiting to get in. They didn't consider me one of their kind, they thought I was from Jerusalem.

The locals knew better. To them, I was a brightly plumaged bird tangled up in the Old City's net, odd and conspicuous. Once I'd been able to move about from one quarter to the other as I chose; now I was really like the Jerusalemites who, for better or worse, were stuck in the Muslim Quarter, or the Armenian, or the Jewish. For the moment, I could still go everywhere, but cautiously, furtively, sneaking through the narrow streets deliberately walking past the police station by the windowless wall. I carried Anahita's bouquet out in front of me like a shield. Every step I took was a torment of hope and fear. The city had simply become unlivable for me.

The convent street was quiet and forbidding as it always is, no matter what time of day. From Anahita's roof garden it doesn't seem at all unfriendly, only sad in its desolation. The stretch between here and Chabad Street, where the sun is friendly and the tourists clamor, is a narrow, stealthy zone, like a belt of no-man's-land around a besieged city. Dirty water flows in the gutters, and something seems to lurk in the silence.

At the crossing someone stood in the shadows. I thought I recognized him but the sun was glaring into my face and I couldn't be sure. He was lean, with a shock of black hair standing straight up. He seemed to be waiting and looked like he'd been there for a long time. I heard a mumble and felt his eyes on me, but when I turned toward him and said "Yassin?" he disappeared into a dark archway. Afterward I couldn't swear that I'd really seen anyone, and I might have been wrong about his appearance. How many times had I actually seen Yassin, Sivan's assistant, as he'd introduced himself? Maybe it was my longing for Sivan conjuring up a mirage.

And what if it was him? Was it coincidence or did he have something to tell me? Had they told him to follow me? But why? Had Sivan sent him? Maybe they wanted to get rid of me. Maybe they were chasing me into someone's arms. But whose? And who was doing the chasing?

Anahita's boutique was closed, the steel gate pulled across the door. Tourists were going in and out of the other stores, which were all open. Her neighbor, a pale, delicate Orthodox Jew weighed down by a big black hat, sold phylacteries and embroidered prayer shawls. He didn't know where she was, but he'd give her the flowers if she came back that day. Otherwise he'd take them home and put them in water, I could depend on it. A Yiddish accent tinted his lilting German; his mother came from Vienna, he told me, but he was born in England.

Now I was scared of Yassin's ghost—scared enough to feel relief when Jodie came walking toward me with an American who introduced himself as a Born Again Jew. She invited me to spend the weekend with her.

"I'm sorry, I won't be in Jerusalem," I said.

"Where are you going?"

Where the afflicted have gone for five thousand years—to the desert.

A few days ago I was sitting in Independence Park, on a shady hillock which looks out over the park's entrance. I knew I was waiting, hopeful, against all common sense and will. Even Sivan's questionable friends, who'd always seemed to pop up in the park and on the street, had disappeared. I couldn't help waiting; my need was stronger than my resolutions, and the eternal wait had changed me, made me small and humble. In fact, I'd shrunk to fit into the tiny hollow that was Sivan's absence. Waiting for him had absorbed my mind and concentrated my being. I didn't know what else to do.

Suddenly I saw him standing by the water fountain. It had to be him, the light gray shirt, slender build, his swift motion as he bent toward the running water, supple, as if he were ready to bolt. He drank, stopped, and looked up at me. I jumped up and waved and ran down the hill, but he went on his way as if he hadn't seen or recognized me. Maybe it wasn't him after all.

The same thing happened several times a day. I'd lean out the hotel window sure that the man below was Sivan. Sometimes the counterfeit was so true that I'd call down to him. At night, I'd dream of him. We'd be in a foreign country, somewhere I'd never been before, making our way through the undergrowth in a Muslim cemetery. The gravestones were tangled in thickets of pine and without warning, they'd swallow Sivan, pulling him down with their twisting roots.

"Don't even try to make sense of it," Nurit once said, speaking of Oriental mysticism. "It possesses the encrypted poetry of a fairy tale. It's like an intense, seductive dream from which you never want to awake."

Or a hideous nightmare you cannot shake off.

"You think in abstractions," she said. "But we Orientals think in pictures and allegories." I believed her then; I don't any more. I was an abstraction for Sivan; he used me as one. He may well have fallen in love with me, to his misfortune. It may well have been that once we were in Ramallah he couldn't resolve the conflict between his love for me and the abstraction that I was and so he fled. At the heart of Nurit's Oriental fairy tale is a wild ferocity akin to the tension that hovers over the city in the heat of the day, when the church bells ring and the muezzin adds his call to prayer. Holy, yes, but savage, too.

Sivan tried to persuade me that his people, whoever they were, had more insight than Westerners, that they lived closer to the truth of themselves. But Sivan had neither deeper insight nor greater compassion. If he spoke in pictures he did so to mislead and evade, and to make himself inaccessible. The pictures he drew were beautiful, seductive, but invariably they dissolved into mist—I could neither verify nor reconstruct them. A new Sivan rose before me. A Sivan who preys on women who've lost their way in the heat of the desert and the sensuousness of the souk, telling them what they want to hear. "You are beautiful," he says. "You are looking for something." A Sivan who swoops down on women who've been hungering for love for years, women who embrace the souk because life at home has long since lost all passion. In their gratitude, they become young and beautiful; they don't think to ask "why me?" They can't imagine that their ardent lover despises them because he's used to despising foreign women, as if they're whores turning tricks for free. And after a while the contempt begins to rub off. I too came to despise the tourist women with their foolish smiles, steered through the street by their young lovers like shiny trophies everyone knows are worthless.

It couldn't happen to me. I know that I'd have sensed the contempt. No, what we had, Sivan and I, contradicted all probability. It was the exception to the rule.

IV

After our journey to Ramallah we spent two more days and one night together. I had begun to miss Sivan even before he left; I just wasn't aware of it.

To me, those two days were like an extended farewell in which we began to hate each other out of sheer despair. Our weeks together had raised many questions and now it was too late to fill in the gaps. Sivan didn't know anything about me, either. In Ramallah he'd found out my real name and age and that I didn't have an American passport but said nothing.

Ever since our first night on the Mount of Olives he had talked about how much he wanted to spend a whole night together in a real bed.

"Come stay with me at the hotel," I'd often said.

"Not here, not in Jerusalem, I don't want to make trouble for you."

"Where else can we go?"

"Somewhere outside the city."

I'd suggested Tel Aviv but he looked at me horrified and no more was said.

Ya'akov claimed he had contacts at the international hotels on the Tel Aviv beach where people couldn't care less about the guests' comings and goings. "A big discount," he promised, "absolutely rock bottom, an insider's price, I'll call you back." He didn't call, but we went anyway, late in the afternoon after we'd returned the rental car as if nothing out of the ordinary had happened.

"Do you know Tel Aviv?" I asked Sivan.

"No, not very well." His eyes were uneasy with fear he was straining to hide.

"It's only forty-five minutes from Jerusalem. If we don't find a room we can come right back."

He looked away from me, obviously under stress, but allowing himself to be persuaded. "Let's take the shuttle taxi, then we can avoid the central bus station," he said.

That way he could take a seat at the last minute, once he'd assured himself that the other passengers were harmless commuters.

He slept during the entire trip, his head sank onto my shoulder. In Tel Aviv he let me walk on ahead to ask the way, as if he'd suddenly lost his tongue. He seemed tense, twitchy, about to bolt at any moment, but I sensed that he was being very courageous.

I checked the strip of hotels along the beach while Sivan waited for me on a low wall in his usual crouching posture. It didn't take long to find out that we weren't going to get a room.

"No vacancies. We'll have to go back to Jerusalem," I said. "I'm sorry." Sivan's face relaxed.

"Huh. Is that big shot with the hotel reservations Jewish?" he wanted to know.

I nodded.

"I thought so." He squeezed my hand as if to say that *he* would never leave me in the lurch like that.

During the ride from Jerusalem to Tel Aviv and back we didn't talk about Ramallah. Once back in Jerusalem Sivan charged ahead. "Follow me, I've done this before," he said.

"Why are we going to Zichron Moshe?" I shouted after him when I realized we were heading for a small residential neighborhood. I wanted to find somewhere busy and anonymous where I wouldn't feel embarrassed at the reception desk. In a place like Zichron Moshe our differences would be hard to ignore.

We turned into the dark entrance of a shabby building and climbed a narrow stairway to the fourth floor. "They're Orthodox Jews here but that doesn't matter," he explained. His identity card lay next to my passport on the reception desk. I recognized the photo but I couldn't read the printed words. He'd already seen my passport. We each put down forty shekels and the bearded man behind the desk gave us a brief, impersonal look. The hotel was full of Russian immigrants. Children in diapers spilled from open doors into a dingy hallway painted green.

I haughtily ignored the ogling stares, but I could imagine the picture I presented: dusty tourist hefting luggage, disheveled after a long day seeing the sights, followed by a Palestinian boy carrying nothing but his identity card. The difference in our age and background slapped my face like a neon light. We were a dirty joke come alive.

In our room the sheet lay twisted on the bed just the way the last occupant had left it. A stiff, gray blanket was tangled on the floor at its foot, ringlets of black hair stuck to the sink, and the mattress was spotted with damp patches.

"There's no way that I'm going to sleep on that mattress," I said.

"I'll see what I can do, maybe they'll give us another one." But Sivan returned humbled and angry.

"What did they say?" I asked.

"Nothing you want to hear."

Whatever it had been, he hated me for it. He looked like a scolded child feeling vengeful. We stood across from each other, embarrassed by the sudden intimacy created by our new privacy, but we felt no desire.

"Let's get something to eat," Sivan suggested.

We were happy to leave the room. I expected a full night together would include a slow meal out in the open air, nothing rushed, just talking, feeling the time passing, knowing we had hours until morning. But Sivan ran down the street without looking back. "Wait," I shouted, but he'd already made his way across Jaffa Road while I was caught at the traffic light. When I was finally able to cross I saw him up ahead at the pedestrian mall, weaving his way through the shoppers and tourists and I choked on angry disappointment.

"Why are you in such a hurry?" I called after him. "We have all night."

"Pizza?" Sivan asked tersely, barely turning his head. While we were waiting for our pizza to heat up he seemed to run in place, throwing quick glances to all sides. Maybe he was looking for that little English girl. Had he been seeing her? The bile that filled my mouth with the sudden stab of mistrust put paid to the gesture of closeness I'd been about to offer.

"Let's sit down," I repeated, but he was already trotting down the street toward the boarding house, a slice of hot pizza in each hand. "I want to sit down!" I shouted.

"We can't!" he yelled back.

"Why not?"

"They'll arrest you if they catch you eating pizza."

I'd never understood his humor and didn't much like it. He laughed at his own joke. "Idiot," I called out, but maybe he wasn't really joking, only making an oblique reference to the trouble I could cause him.

Had Ya'akov appeared at that moment I would have let Sivan go his own way. I was desperate for food and conversation, to sit in peace without being stared at by small-minded nosy gossips, to talk without stalling over each word, to delight in a challenging discussion when you feel as though you're really grappling with the thoughts in someone else's head. Nurit, Eli, even Anahita—but not Sivan.

I walked blindly through the crowd. I felt lost, unmoored, with no connection to the people out enjoying a balmy evening and no control over my own actions. I was still able to sound a faint note of resistance, but my strength was fading fast. At the boarding house, we closed the blue window shutters to block out the sight of our neighbors across the alley, not an arm's length away. We could see them sitting under a dim light bulb at their half-cleared dining table.

Sivan and I sat at the edge of the bed, careful not to touch each other. We ate and then did what we had come to do, but we had waited too long for this privacy. There was no talk between our embraces, as if we'd lost interest in learning about each other. The knowledge wouldn't have done us much good, anyway.

"Tell me something," I whispered. "Why don't you like Jews?"

"I like you," he said tenderly. "A lot."

"But why?" I persisted. If he told me nothing else, I wanted to understand that one thing.

"Look at what they've done to the Palestinians," he said, struggling with his reluctance to take up my question.

"But not all of them, and the Arabs are making things difficult, too." I had wanted a simple answer, not a political discussion.

"We've been living in a state of war," he said, "for as long as I can remember."

"Why do you identify with the Arab side so much?"

"I went to their schools and they're my friends. I live with them."

"And so what? You think their terror is right?"

"It's complicated," he said wearily and turned away from me, pretending to sleep. But when I touched him, he closed his arms around me, enfolding me in his warmth, as if at least in sleep he could beat back that which kept us apart.

In the morning we were in a hurry to get out. Children played noisily in the hallway, the shower was broken, and by the light of day the room was even more repulsive. I watched Sivan get dressed—so much beauty in one man—and wanted to hold him to me forever.

"Could you fasten my necklace?" It was a chain I wear, mostly beneath my clothes, a six-pointed star of antiqued silver. I had found it among the folded handkerchiefs in my mother's chest. It had slipped between two gaping joints and owed its survival to my nosiness. I watched the concentration on Sivan's face, the way he struggled with the filigree clasp. He was so close that I could feel his breath on my neck. When he let the necklace go, a barely concealed smirk of triumph flitted across his lips, the kind of mischievous delight that comes with pulling off a prank.

I went to say good-bye to Nurit. We drove up to see the spectacular views from the Haas Promenade, high above the city in the east. "I want to show you Jerusalem at its very best," she said. Stretched out before us, baking in the white heat, the city was circled by a ring of new stone buildings with which it seemed to have nothing in common. The wind started to lift Nurit's curls, but they were too heavy. "I wish I could make you a present of the city," she said. "I wish you could find peace here, though maybe you have to live somewhere else for a while. I know you'll be back."

"Maybe not."

"Of course you will, you can't help it. You're one of us, an addict. You'll come back, and one of these days you'll stay. But I'm leaving."

"You're going? Where?"

"India. I've been studying Sanskrit for a long time. I'm an Oriental, I've told you. Israel's too Western for me. I don't know how to think about Israel and the Palestinians and the Intifada. I say things and think things I'm ashamed of. I'd rather belong to neither side. I haven't been to the Old City for more than a year. I used to go every day. After school we'd sit in the coffee houses feeling completely comfortable. Not any more. Now I'm too ashamed to go."

"So you think things are simpler in India? Why, because you're not responsible for what happens there? Do you remember telling me that people here see the world as one poetic whole, that they don't use other people for their own purposes. Well, you were wrong. Someone used me and then just left."

"I know, the Armenian."

"What do you know?"

"Nothing in particular, I've just been watching you. It could be that he just got bored. Not everything is political. The truth is that we live banal, trivial lives in which we come together out of boredom and leave each other out of boredom."

"And some people get involved in politics out of boredom and kill people along the way, but apart from that they're entirely normal, with the same capacity for love as everyone else."

"Devorah, I think you should go home for a while. You sound really hurt. Stop tormenting yourself and stop beating yourself up." And then Nurit told me about the Vedic myth. When young women are overcome by passion, they run into the wild. With the strength of their aching desire they beat the trees until they begin to bloom, but the blossoms give off no scent.

"All creation has an element of violence," Nurit said. "A kind of cruel beauty. There's no need to fear it, even if you lose control."

For a moment, I was tempted to spill the whole story, but I was too tired and let my thoughts drift away into the desert. Jerusalem was a long way off, it nestled small and chalky in the scorched hills. Did it really matter so much? From this distance, Sivan, Ramallah, me—it all began to lose significance.

I left Nurit at her bookshop. "Don't say good-bye," she said. "You'll see me again."

I rented a car at a different agency. Everything went very smoothly. The young woman placed the carbon paper over my credit card—the same card I used to pay for the other car—and pulled the roller across it. I signed and the vehicle was waiting for me by the sidewalk. If anyone were to look for me, they could easily trace my license number. No more efforts to hide my tracks. I'd broken through the thin crust of reality into the twilight of persecution; now I gave up the conviction that I could control what they knew or what they did. At two-thirty I rented a beige Fiat Uno with Israeli plates. Then I picked up my luggage at my hotel, paid in shekels, left East Jerusalem via Nablus Street, and headed toward Jericho. If someone was taking note, so be it. It wasn't my job to work out what it all meant. Let them explain it to me. Since Ramallah my movements and decisions, no matter how spontaneous, no longer belonged just to me.

I'd driven halfway to the Jordan Valley when I turned off at Wadi Kilt. It was the first time I'd gone along this stretch of road without Sivan next to me. Absolute solitude has within it a great simplicity, in harmony with the desert. For the first time in weeks, I wasn't waiting for something. I was alone on the brown desert slopes, in a wasteland of stone and sand. The parched wadi lay beneath me at dizzying depths, half-filled with a blue shadow that would slowly climb the opposite slope. The sharp desert winds and the rains of winter had cut grooves and terraces into the slopes, as if a stonemason had been carving a fortress out of the desert and had left a waste of finely pulverized sand on the desert floor below. And suddenly, a turn, and Jericho came into sight, with its blinding sun, palm trees, banana groves, mangos, and the unbridled red of fire trees.

I drove past the roadblock without slowing down or speeding up. The soldier in the guardhouse rested his rifle across his knees and didn't bother to look up.

In the primitive cafeteria at the intersection of Jerusalem and the Dead Sea I ate supper. The two Palestinians behind the counter acted as if they hadn't noticed me. "Hummus and pita," I said. Their impassive faces didn't waver but one of them began, ever so sluggishly, to fill a flat plastic plate with hummus and poured olive oil in it, while the other man stared out at the desert as if in a trance. A very young soldier with no sign of facial hair stumbled in, the glass door closing heavily behind him. "Tahini," he said in a gentle almost pleading voice. The two behind the counter didn't look up at him, either. One of them passed him the plate, raised his head, and looked right past the soldier with expressionless eyes, as if he too were transfixed by the desert. I spent half an hour at one of the sticky Formica tables. Not one word was spoken the entire time. Only the fan hummed.

It's as hard for them to let the word "Israeli" pass their lips as it was for Alvin to let the word "Jew" pass his. Mostly, Palestinians say "they" when they're talking about Israelis, and Israelis say "they" too, meaning the others, the enemy. I'm a third category, Sivan had told me.

I continued south, past the palm orchard where Sivan and I had stopped. The palms were too far away from the road to provide any shade, but we'd pulled over just for the joy of knowing that no one could see us. We were alone there, the desert belonged to everyone. No one and everyone was alien here, neither of us had an advantage. Still, we'd spoken softly to hear the silence between our sentences. In the end, we'd only really spoken in the desert, free of Sivan's restlessness, his rage that would flare so abruptly and then wane just as fast. "The thing I like about you," he said, "is that you don't always have to talk, and sometimes you even hear things that aren't said."

But being with him was a kind of exercise in asceticism. It's so hard not to betray yourself when you talk. Most sentences begin with "I" and then you've already said a lot, and the other person might want to know how and why and when. Before you know it, your line of retreat has narrowed, and then the things that were yours no longer belong to you. I could sense his feelings but he never gave me the facts, and you can't depend on feeling alone. For the most part I was traveling with a stranger.

"Do you like music?" I asked him. It was a simple question, but he had no use for it.

"What are you getting at?" he said.

"I'm not trying to get at anything, I'm just trying to find out what you like. Maybe I like the same things."

"Do you read?" was another question.

"All the time," he said. "I have to clip the editorials out of the newspapers every day, and there are a lot of newspapers in this country."

"Why do you do that? Is it part of your job?" I asked.

Unnerved, he clammed up. He'd already said too much, and he probably wouldn't have said that much had he not heard the condescension in my voice. "You are intelligent," it said. "Why don't you make something of yourself?"

"What do you do in your free time?" was the first question I'd asked him.

"Why? Nothing special. Annoy the tourists. It's so easy to get a rise out of them." He showed me how to swear in seven languages.

"Why don't you go to university?" I asked him.

"It's pointless. The schools on the West Bank are closed most of the time, and even if I graduated I wouldn't get a job."

"So you just hang out."

"I don't hang out, I make money," he said, obviously offended. "I'm doing more with my life than you are with yours."

"In what way? Why do you think that?"

"Because you're only living for yourself."

I had told him nothing about myself, not my age, not my real name, only that I lived in New York, but not for how long. I'd mentioned that I spent a lot of time in libraries and that I'd made several successful documentaries. I talked about the seasons on the east coast, about Indian summers and the heavy snowfall in winter, and the Jewish holidays I spent with my friends, but I got the impression that he wasn't really interested in anything I told him. I saw contempt in his face. "You're so proud of yourself," his look said. Sometimes he seemed to despise me, as if I was a spoiled, shallow person who didn't really know a thing about life. I couldn't share the things I loved with him, he simply wasn't interested.

After our one night together we parted at Jaffa Road, tired, unwashed, with empty stomachs. I looked for shelter for the coming night and then ate breakfast in the deserted garden of a kosher restaurant, alone, far from the street.

We both knew that the end was coming, but I closed my eyes to it. Our love had been a battle against hate and suspicion, but the more love and hate became entangled, the more fiercely we were convinced of our feelings for each other.

That afternoon I saw Sivan from a long way off. He was waiting for me at the usual place and he looked dispirited and tired. He didn't see me until I was standing in front of him. I had come from an unexpected direction and it frightened him to see me there suddenly.

Maybe Ramallah had put him at great risk; to be seen with me could be suicidal lunacy. His mission was finished and had failed: Following orders, he had lured me to Ramallah to turn me over to his comrades, and then thought better of it. I pretended not to notice that something had changed. All we had left was our love and our doubts about each other, but our love was an unwanted obstacle that should never have happened.

Sivan stood up, lit a cigarette as we began walking, took a puff, and threw it away. The black stubble he hadn't shaved since Ramallah made his face look older.

"Something's happened," he said.

"What?"

"I can't tell you here, wait until we're alone."

Putting several paces between us, he walked in broad strides to Independence Park.

"What is it?" I asked again, as we sat down on the parched grass.

"Do you love me?" he asked, abruptly.

I looked at him, startled, his voice sounded tormented, almost angry. "You know that I do," I said. "Do you love me?"

"Of course, would I be here if I didn't? Do you want to meet my family?"

"Why?" I asked, in order not to say no. I could imagine his family—parents most likely my age, curious brothers and sisters, and their dismay: "What are you doing with that woman? Who is she?" Maybe they'd already chosen a girl for him, someone from the neighborhood with a gentle face and shy, downcast eyes.

He didn't repeat his offer, but looked at me with a mute gaze that seemed to carry a stream of urgent messages that I could not decipher. He stroked my hair in the sunlight and stared at it as if he were trying to fix it in his mind.

We sat this way for a long while, looking at each other, the way a person looks at a scene he's about to leave forever. The evening grew dark, the grass became damp, and we moved deeper into the park. On a bench among the bushes I shivered and Sivan held me close.

"Take me back with you," he begged.

"I can't, you know I can't."

An Orthodox Jew rode by on his bicycle, taking his time to move on.

"Then stay here with me. I'll rent a house in East Jerusalem."

I shook my head. In East Jerusalem, I thought, horrified. How could he want to do something like that to me, keep me cooped up and cut off from everything I know? I remembered how a woman in Vienna had once asked me whether I'd ever move to Israel. "Why not," I'd said. She'd been dismayed—"There are just Jews there, I mean, no other people. If you live where everyone's the same, then you have to think like they do." "I'm Jewish," I said, and left her standing alone, embarrassed.

"New immigrants get everything," Sivan said bitterly. "Apartments, money, jobs—you can immigrate, you're Jewish."

I didn't say a word.

Directly behind us in the bushes something was moving.

"Stay here," Sivan whispered, "I'll check it out, don't look in my direction no matter what you hear." In the darkness, I heard him speak Arabic. He came back and kissed me hard, his lit cigarette near my head.

"We love each other, we have to stay together," he pleaded.

"You're young," I said, as if I were talking to an obstinate child. "You're Armenian, you'll marry an Armenian girl. I'm Jewish."

"To hell with the Jews!" he said. The Orthodox man rode back on his bicycle and gave us a threatening look. I put my hand over Sivan's mouth.

"To hell with the Armenians!" he yelled, pulling my hand away from his mouth. Terrified, I looked into a face tortured by agonizing hatred. He was always so controlled, never more than the briefest burst of smoldering violence, never a loud word, never a loss of restraint, not even in love.

A thin, seedy-looking man with matted hair appeared out of nowhere, every inch one of the pimps Nurit had warned me about. They hung around the bushes with watchful eyes and from time to time they'd saunter up to someone as if by chance, exchange a few words, and ask for the time or a light. They live in the park like crows in a newly sown field. They all look the same with their wolfish faces and wiry, ageless bodies whose movements are indefinably obscene. The man stared at us aggressively and was in no hurry to go on his way.

"Fuck the Jews!" Sivan screamed for everyone to hear.

"Let's go," I pleaded, "people are looking at us."

"It doesn't matter where we go, we're always being watched," he said.

We went to Mamilla, to the cemetery, but someone was sitting by the path as if he'd been waiting for us.

"You are my sunshine," Sivan began to sing and held me so tightly that it hurt.

"Are we really being followed?" I asked in his ear. "Is it because of the car?"

"Shut up," he growled at me, and loudly began to sing some Israeli hit about unrequited love. He had a husky melodic voice. That evening we found nowhere to be alone. Even the margins, the places where we'd always felt safe from prying eyes, were now occupied, as if the city was pushing us out.

In Independence Park the voyeurs had turned into predators. At Sultan's Pool preparations were underway for the summer festival. In the landscaped gardens adjoining the big hotels elaborate water sprinklers discouraged lovers and backpackers from camping under the trees in the dark. For a while, we sat in the shadow of a large sculpture behind the King David Hotel, but even there Sivan kept hearing whispers and footsteps. He'd go to check them out, as if confronting his pursuers, and each time he came back even more frightened.

"Tell me what really happened in Ramallah," I said.

"What's to tell? You were there."

"Why did your friend drive through the roadblock?"

"I told you, we didn't have driver's licenses." Sivan's voice had turned hostile and brusque and as we walked he pushed me up so close to the wall with its overhanging branches that I had to keep ducking to avoid being hit in the face. There was a new ferocity in his touch and in his words that scared me. As we continued on our interminable quest, on our aimless search for shelter, I saw him turn into someone else, someone brutal who was deaf to my pleas.

"I asked a friend," I said. "She thinks there's more to it than a missing license."

"You told an Israeli?" Sivan grabbed my shoulders with both hands, a murderous panic in his eyes. "Just what did you tell her?"

"Just about the checkpoint."

He let go and ran ahead of me. I tried to catch up.

On King David Street he started talking to women, asking them the time. "Hello," he said. "Where are you going?" he asked. "Can I come? I like you."

I waited off to the side as if I'd decided to see how much humiliation I could take. When Sivan was finished, he pushed me through an imposing wooden doorway etched with the ten commandments. "We're going in here, you first."

"Are you crazy?" I hissed. "This is a synagogue." But he was gone, feverishly seeking something ahead, an invisible grail. He dragged me along, tormenting me, and I let him, without protest. I don't understand why I did, but I burn with shame to think that someone else saw my disgrace that night, that we might have been followed all the way back to the Muslim cemetery where we made love one last time, quickly and without tenderness, as if Sivan had to erase every recollection of past joy.

We both thought he was there, our silent observer, and Sivan showed him what they do with Jewish women. "Fuck the Jews," he'd screamed in their faces. It was a rare triumph over his powerlessness.

"So you say you were kidnapped in your own car," I imagine the observer saying, "which then crashed an army checkpoint, driven by this mechanic from Ramallah. Why didn't you report it immediately?"

"I couldn't betray my lover."

"That's not an answer. Instead, you put other lives at risk, the lives of innocent people. There may well have been a bomb in the car."

That's betrayal, too. It's worse than betrayal, it's treason. I've exiled myself from the community I wanted to belong to for so long. Treason deserves expulsion.

We both knew we were causing each other to commit treachery. We loved all the more passionately for it and hated all the more desperately.

On Hillel Street, Sivan hailed a taxi, shoved me into the back seat and shouted my hotel address to the driver. "What are you doing?" I called to him. "I'll decide whether I need a taxi." But he was out of earshot, running toward the Old City.

"But you met him the next day, did you not?"

Yes I did. I went to our meeting place and he was there, that is, he came late, which was unusual. It was the last evening before his disappearance.

The large red disk of sun melted into the chain of mountains over the Dead Sea. I had wanted to reach the kibbutz in time for the sunset, but I had gotten lost in the dizzying desert curves and the evening had grown sad and heavy. After each right-hand turn I saw the sea beneath me, velvet blue with a violet rim where the Jordanian mountains met the water. The inaccessibly remote mountain range seemed to float above the shore.

This is the second station in my pilgrimage, the Dead Sea an hour after sunset when light drains from the heavens. It's a peculiar compulsion, this need to be here at exactly the right moment, with my face turned to Jordan as if in supplication. I saw it with Gilbert, with Sivan from the steep bank of a thirsty wadi, and many times alone. I was even here with Alvin, but sea and shore had melded into a washed-out pink and

I felt cheated of my moment. When we met in the ardent first green of a European spring I'd told him that we would go to the Dead Sea in autumn and sleep there as the sun set. But then we forgot, and the next year it was too late, we no longer even touched hands.

On a mountaintop, as the last of the light faded, I climbed out of the car. The milky sea lay far below, streaked with dark blue. The Jordanian range had almost completely disappeared behind a fine veil of haze, but all around me, heavy and steep, stood the mountains of the Judean desert, their gouged cliffs turning from flaming copper to a dull reddish brown, losing luminosity by the minute. Then they gave themselves over to the colors of the night and like huge animals with their large humped backs, they lay themselves down.

The metallic sheet of the water's surface reflected the moonlight, making a quicksilver track between the shores, and the night winds brought with them an intense loneliness. I fled to the kibbutz guesthouse, where an echo of desert stillness hung over every room, soothing and a little melancholy.

"A single room?" the girl at the reception desk asked. "Would you like coffee?" Something about me seemed to elicit her sympathy.

"Yes, and a big bar of chocolate," I answered. We smiled. Maybe she thought I was fleeing a personal misery. If so, she was right. But I felt comfortable here on the mountaintop above the Dead Sea, safe and out of danger for the first time in many weeks. I had found a sanctuary.

In my room, I heard the wind tearing at the trees and the dry palm branches scraping the roof overhead. As the wind raged and rolled, I was warm in my berth, as if in a sturdy ship on a stormy sea. This place was not just another station in my journey but its end; I felt as if here on this mountaintop, fenced in by barbed wire left from the Yom Kippur War, with goats dotting the slopes, I was protected from the future, even from myself and my immoderate desires. I felt like the crazy woman I saw in Safed, dancing awkwardly to the rhythm of drums in the middle of a courtyard, twisting her gaunt, emaciated body in her yearning for tenderness. And I understood, if only for a moment, Nurit's composure, and the calm self-assurance of the women in East Jerusalem. Only then did I realize that were I to stay in Israel I would have to learn restraint, acceptance.

Years ago, in the kibbutz at Ashkelon, I thought I'd mastered a life without the pressure of time, savoring the lazy afternoons, the hours between sleeping and waking, the tranquil Saturdays in the shade of the eucalyptus on the beach. But not a year had passed before I couldn't stand it and now, above the Dead Sea, the night was just beginning and the storm was still raging, stirring up sand squalls, but I was already restless and ready to move on in the morning. When I climbed into bed the fear took over and the interrogation resumed. "What do you remember?"

"A hundred different things, incidents, moments, which seemed insignificant at the time. I forgot about them until now. I can see new meanings that I should've understood all along. How could I have been so blind?"

Once, I asked Sivan when his birthday was, a question most people answer without a second thought. But he did a whole string of calculations. Apparently he was translating from one chronology to another. "I'm Virgo," he said. September, I guessed, or the end of August. But that only seemed to make it more complicated. I tried the Jewish calendar, Elul, Tishri? But that proved even less useful. In which calendar was he at home, in which reality? He came into my life from a distant planet; we didn't even share a calendar.

"On the fifteenth of September," he said, finally, and was relieved, as if he had just solved a difficult problem in his head.

Who was he, really, and where had he gone? Did his nervousness and the vigilance in his eyes come from a willingness to die at any moment? From a brutal life with his back against the wall? But then again, he was cheerful, and his enthusiasm surprised me again and again. Life was less serious when I was with him; not every moment had to be meaningful. "Let's drive to the desert," he'd say, "and smoke something, I've got a little hashish." "I can't," I'd say. "I can't drive when I'm hallucinating." He wanted to live hard and love hard, recklessly, every day.

Sivan became less and less willing to make plans in advance. He never knew when he'd be free. Plans were made in the early evening, according to a sense of time in which the day began once the sun had set. The next day was a void, an unpredictable future. In the interim he had to live fast as if there were no future for which to save himself.

"You smoke too much," I said. "You're cutting years off your life."

He grinned.

Except for one short moment, in the desert, when my car began to rock and sway beneath us, it was impossible to imagine him killing in cold blood. But on the drive back he had been so considerate, and before that, so gentle and caring, I rejected the idea, and focused on the man who was with me. The hatred which sometimes broke out of him was always quickly brought under control. In West Jerusalem he opened the car door and hurriedly threw out aluminum cans and empty water bottles as if they were explosives. "Keep your country clean," he said, while he was tossing them out, and his biting, disproportionate scorn was aimed at me. Practice for his mission? But who had trained him? Did he belong to a group or just hate in a freelance kind of way?

"Terror is an art to be learned," Sivan had once said, very casually, correcting my terminology. I had been talking about political activism and that had led to a disagreement about the terms "freedom fighter" and "terrorist." What level had he attained by the time I lost sight of him? What was his rank in the hierarchy, this intelligent young man who spoke four languages? Yassin had introduced himself as Sivan's assistant, his subordinate. So did he lead the men in Ramallah? Was my kidnapping a kind of trial run for him, his graduation ceremony? Had he accidentally fallen in love while he was supposed to have remained cold-blooded? And was he now being punished for fraternizing with the enemy? Was there a term for it, despicable and unforgiving, like "Racial Debasement"? What was the point of his skill at initiating relationships, if he couldn't extricate himself as the need arose?

Sivan had talked me into renting a car. I had actually wanted to take the bus to Safed. I'm sure it had all been well prepared in advance; the cell in Ramallah had received word, the house was selected, the victim so blinded that she was willing to walk right into the trap. And then he rescued me after he'd offered me up. Or had it all been really quite harmless? Was I having paranoid delusions? Taken one by one, the events seemed so reasonable that it's hard to say when exactly things got out of hand. The whole only became visible to me much later. New memories surface every day. And with each one Sivan becomes more and more of an enigma. Before long, I'll be asking myself whether he ever existed.

The day we drove up to Ramallah I'd arranged to meet Nurit. We sat in a café at a tiny white table under the cascading branches of a laurel which kept getting tangled in our hair. We were both distracted and irritable. Nurit told me about a bad dream she had had, and seemed intent on spreading gloom and creating an atmosphere full of evil portent. In a way, her vulnerability to signs and fleeting anxieties reminded me of Sivan. From time to time, she looked into my eyes, full of suspicion, and held my gaze as if she were trying to extract some secret I was withholding from her.

"I can tell what people are thinking," she said, "but I'd rather not know, it makes my life difficult."

I told her about the car and that Sivan, the Armenian, had said his friend could repair it.

"Is the mechanic Israeli?" she wanted to know.

"I don't think so."

"Then be careful."

We changed the subject. She vehemently rejected the unspoken reproach that she was a bigot.

"I haven't been in East Jerusalem for a long time," she said. "I don't like to come to their impoverished homes well-dressed and embarrass them. One day there will be a border and I can go as a tourist, with my passport."

I was appalled. "And the Old City, the Western Wall?"

"For you, Jerusalem as a symbol is holier than the people who live there," she said, with irony. "The wall is a pile of old rocks, and a flag is nothing but a scrap of cloth. Only people are holy. I know I'm not very patriotic."

Neither one of us felt much like talking. We were both restless and couldn't stick with any one topic for very long.

On the way back to Zion Square, an old man sitting on a stool in front of an open door cursed us for smoking in the street. I had just thrown a cigarette butt into the gutter. I vacillated between defiance and a bad conscience and grew stubborn, as if I'd picked up some of the hate Sivan expressed when he threw soda cans into the street. I'd been jolted out of the euphoria of belonging, without knowing how or why. In an instant I felt isolated from everyone, a feeling I knew well, isolated from myself and an outrage to everyone else. To the old man, I must have looked like an insensitive tourist without the least sense of tact and consideration. Like someone who had no business being in Jerusalem.

I went back to pick up the cigarette butt.

"Excuse me," I said, and he nodded graciously.

"Ignore him," Nurit said. "He's just a grumpy old man."

By four o'clock, I was back in my room looking out at the stone facade of the house across the way, at its blue wrought-iron balcony with its bulges and flourishes and the water dripping from the air conditioners protruding from darkened windows. In one window, directly across from mine, two Sabbath candles were lit every Friday evening, and sometimes a white sheet hung out over the windowsill like an offer of peace or surrender.

I looked down at passersby and saw only their hair, their shoulders, and what they were carrying in their hands. Often they stopped and called to each other across the street, exchanging words with shopkeepers who were out of my line of vision. Only later, after six o'clock, did they begin to walk more purposefully, on their way back home from work. I tried to guess by their haircuts and hats, by the color of their clothing, where they lived, in which quarter. I became impatient. It was close to seven o'clock and the sun had left the street. My heart began to beat harder and my armpits grew moist with perspiration.

Nothing had prepared me for the turmoil in my body when I thought of Sivan, when I waited for him and knew that he'd soon be standing before me with his ironic grin, the dimples at the corners of his mouth, and the large black eyes which had missed me all day. At least, that's what I thought I read in his eager face. Several times my pulse would race and my temples would pound, but the young man below would walk under my window oblivious to the trouble he was causing. Then my pulse would slow and make itself felt instead as a deep longing. I hadn't waited for anyone with as much anticipation since I was a teenager.

At seven-thirty, he called without saying his name.

"I am in the telephone booth on the corner, come down, we're waiting."

Yassin and another burly Palestinian were waiting with Sivan a few feet from the hotel, looking at me and grinning suggestively.

"Can you give me a picture of yourself," he'd once asked, "but I'd like one taken a few years go, when you were younger."

"So you can brag to your friends?"

"Yes, that's right," he admitted.

The men were standing together like a pack of conspirators and I could see the distance in Sivan's eyes. I felt abandoned. I was being coolly appraised and it made me uneasy.

"Let's go to the car."

At some point I yielded my will to his, but I don't know exactly when that was. While we were walking to the car? On the way to the parking lot where the dark, heavy man crawled under the car with a screwdriver in his hand? When I accepted Sivan's terse decree that we would have to take the car to Ramallah, to a real repair shop to get it fixed?

"Kidnapped? Did they force you into the car? In the middle of Jerusalem? Did you put up a fight? Did you ask where they were taking you? Why did you let the man who called himself Sivan simply take the car key, without putting up a struggle, and then watch him give it to a complete stranger?"

I obediently climbed into the back seat. Yassin got in next to the dark man in front, and Sivan sat next to me like a stranger. He did not touch me at all, not even with a finger, not even with his eyes.

"Where are we going," I asked timidly. By that time, we were taking the road out of East Jerusalem.

Yassin lay a red plain *keffiyeh* across the dashboard. I felt anesthetized. It was already getting dark. I think the road was straight but I have no coherent memory of either the drive or what happened later.

The West Bank slipped by as if in a haze. I remember the Beduins' black goatskin tents flapping in the wind. Shredded tires lay along the side of the road, and here and there the charred skeletons of an army truck.

Somewhere along the way, I was overcome by a nightmarish

feeling of unreality which has not left me since. I could not turn to Sivan, he was infinitely distant from me. In the last light of evening the desert stretched barren and forsaken. Now and then a house would appear as we approached a small town, an ornate villa with little towers.

"Ramallah," Sivan said, more to himself than to me. I looked helplessly down at his hands, which were hanging loosely between his knees. He had become unapproachable, inaccessible even through words. I stared at the back of Yassin's head, at his bristly black hair. From time to time, in the rearview mirror, I caught the eyes of the man at the wheel, the mechanic who had been unable to fix my car. His face was impassive and he drove with a kind of urgency. Suddenly I felt like a hostage.

It was dark when we turned off the main road onto a gravel path and stopped in front of a half-finished, one-story concrete block. The car was surrounded by young boys leaning against the windows and hanging from the roof with their hands. They grabbed the door handles and pressed themselves up against the car. I was sure the thin sheet metal was going to buckle under their weight. They stared at me from all sides, neither hostile nor friendly, but with indifference, the way you would study an object. I sat cowering in the corner holding the collar of my blouse tightly closed around my neck, trying to meet their eyes, without hostility or fear, as if there were nothing unusual about the situation.

Sivan was still far away from me, as if none of this were his concern, and he resolutely avoided looking me in the face. Someone reached through the window and handed the dark man some tools. We stopped in front of the building for a long time. Men walked by, threw a quick look my way, and disappeared. While were waiting a tall, brawny man squeezed his way into the car, between me and Sivan.

"Why are we waiting?" I asked, and got no answer.

Finally we drove back to the paved road and through another neighborhood with beautiful old houses, then into a desolate area dotted with the remains of demolished homes, rough concrete walls and deserted gas stations. We stopped before a gate of heavy iron bars, massive as a prison entrance. Yassin got out, slid back one side of the gate, and we drove into the dark courtyard where only the outlines of the buildings were visible.

The dark man held the door open for me and I meekly got out of the car, no longer asking any questions. I did what I was told. I expected nothing and was ready for everything. No matter what happened, I was determined to show neither fear nor surprise.

"They are going to repair your car now," Sivan said, "and we'll take a little walk."

"What's your name?" I asked my new escort, just to create a sense of normalcy.

"Sa'id," he answered. "I am a medical student at Bir Zeit University. Are you a student, too?"

"No," I said.

We went down dark and gloomy streets. All the windows and doorways were shuttered with aluminum grates and iron doors. There was graffiti on the walls and no other human being in sight, as if there were a curfew. I lost all sense of direction and hardly took notice of any of the houses. My fear had given way to numbness. I'll never see the car again, I thought, but even that realization left me cold. Sivan and I kept our distance, as if we'd only just met. I walked through the streets with the two of them, both my arms crossed over my body as if I were trying to fight off the cold.

"Look at this," Sivan said, and for a moment I felt relieved, thinking he was going to talk to me again. But his voice was different, not throaty and soft, with rounded consonants. "Let's bark," is what he said when he wanted me to park the car. "Like a dog?" I once asked, and could see that I had hurt him. "Park," I corrected him, "can you hear the difference?" But he couldn't hear it and again said "bark."

Now his voice was impersonal and hard, as if he were addressing an assembly. Before the deathly still houses of Ramallah he was calling the faithful to rebellion. He delivered his battle cry so well I thought he'd learned it by heart or, at the very least, repeated it many times. In short, harsh sentences, he spoke of Jewish repression and brutality, of expropriated land and demolished houses, even here, in these streets. "Look, just look, will you." Of harassment at the roadblocks, daily humiliations, beatings, jail, many of his friends here in Ramallah were in military prison, not to mention the poverty, the despair, the degradation willfully inflicted. "Look at it!" His gesture took in the whole city, which, in the darkness, seemed little more than a few mournful facades. "A slum, the whole city, one big slum! And they don't fix a thing, all they do is destroy! Why do you think East Jerusalem looks so clean when Ramallah is so rundown?"

I refused him an answer. You're not going to pin that on me, I thought. I kept staring straight ahead with the same defiant look I'd seen on his face whenever I'd mentioned the army or the sacrifices Israel had made for this land.

"Because they want to pull the wool over the tourists' eyes, because they're lying, they're lying to the whole world, and first and foremost to America," he said, answering his own question.

I've seen plenty of slums, I thought, and Ramallah is no slum, neglected perhaps, rundown, but that's your business if you let your cities go to seed. I kept quiet, not because I was scared but to punish him, to leave him twisting in the wind with his rhetorical questions the same way he'd always withdrawn from me and hid behind his contemptuous silence.

"Look!" he shouted pointing to the potholes in the asphalt, to a broken down door, a half-razed wall, a gas station without gas pumps.

I shrugged my shoulders. We were enemies, and the more he blamed me, the less willing I was to listen to him. What did this have to do with me? Hadn't I been gathering opinions for weeks, trying to reach a fair judgment, to listen for positions which held out the promise of resolution? I was outside myself, watching us as we made our way through the streets of Ramallah! Sivan declaiming wildly, the big, burly student who, like me, was silent, me in the middle, my arms crossed trying to keep warm. I was in a play in which all the actors had been told their cues except me. The drive and the disappearance of the car could be elements meant to heighten suspense; Sivan's harangue against the backdrop of the silent city was the climax, meaning the denouement was soon to come. And the medical student? Perhaps the diatribe was for his benefit, not mine. Maybe he stood in for the audience that would evaluate Sivan's call to action. Maybe he was an important person sent to assess Sivan's courage and performance. What else would move Sivan to shout his rage in Ramallah's deathly streets which could well have been under curfew? Sivan, who usually talked as if the whole country were bugged. Careful, a quick look to the left and to the right, his voice low, hand in front of his mouth.

"In there," Sivan said suddenly and, holding me tightly by the elbow, pushed open the door to a house.

Before he dragged me inside, I tried to get an impression of the facade, perhaps as evidence: It was a one-story building with a green wash, plain, no windows at street level; there on the sidewalk stood my car, parked up close to the wall, enjoying the special protection of the house. We went through a long twisting corridor, past closed doors. The house seemed as lifeless as the street outside.

At the end of the hallway, a door opened into a brightly lit room. It seemed we were expected. Yassin and the dark man were sitting on plastic covered chairs facing two other men who sat on a sofa. None of the furniture matched and this was clearly not a room someone lived in. The whitewashed walls were bare except for three photographs of bearded men. I was offered a seat where I was exposed to the resolute gaze of a young man with bushy eyebrows and a red *keffiyeh*. Beneath this picture sat the host himself, who also fixed me in his gaze. He was about fifty and the others treated him with obvious deference.

"He is a musician," the medical student said respectfully.

"Do you speak Hebrew?" he asked.

I shrugged. "A little."

"*Yoffi*, good," he said and grinned. "And Arabic?"

I shook my head.

The men started all talking at once. I recognized a few words, the name of my hotel, Jerusalem street names; at some point I thought they were talking about my passport, about America, New York, Austria. I watched their eyes and their gestures and tried to infer their intentions from their tone. Whatever they were saying, it was clearly about me.

"What are they talking about?" I asked Sivan, who sat near me at the end of the table.

"He was asking me what your name is," was his evasive answer. The others laughed.

"Would you like some tea?" Sivan asked.

I shook my head.

"He was asking you if you'd like some tea," he repeated impatiently.

"No."

"It's impolite to refuse an offer of hospitality," Sivan said. "So, we'll try again. Would you like some tea?"

"Tell him I can't sleep if I drink tea."

He was clearly irritated by my pig-headedness and gave our host a look of exasperation.

The student at my left was leaning back on the shabby sofa. He was smoking and trying to touch my leg with his bare foot. Yassin and the dark one sat on their chairs attentively, watching the scene unfold. The host reached for a stringed instrument and began to play, but he did not let me out of his sight for a moment. He gave me a penetrating look intended to bewitch me while coaxing mournful tones out of his instrument, without melody or rhythm. The student sang along in a high falsetto that sounded like a suppressed howl.

"A love song," Sivan said, and I could feel myself turning red under the gaze of our host. The dark man left the room, then came back a few minutes later. He looked perplexed, demoralized, with his two missing teeth and shaggy hair. There was an undisguised salaciousness in the way he looked at me.

As long as Sivan is here they won't do anything to me, I thought, it's a matter of honor. But then I remembered the story that was in all of the newspapers a few years ago, about a young Irish woman about to board a plane with an explosive in her handbag. She hadn't known a thing about the good-bye present from her fiancé, a Palestinian whose child she was carrying: She was several months pregnant and would have exploded along with the entire plane, clueless right up to the end.

Since the return of the dark man there was a new irritability in the air. They were all talking in loud voices, interrupting each other, and it was obvious that they were arguing about something.

"Please give me your passport," Sivan asked, straining to show an impersonal politeness toward me.

I handed him my passport, my well-guarded secret, and watched him carefully pry open my lies, my half-truths and my silences. I wanted to protest. What does my passport have to do with me, anyway? It's not the truth, it doesn't mean anything. Ten years ago I had a different passport and that wasn't me, either. I outgrew the irrelevant data long ago. My passport is lying, it belongs to someone else.

But I kept still while they shouted at each other and Sivan waved my passport in the air, triumphantly, like a piece of evidence, repeating the same sentence over and over again. Finally I figured out what he was saying. "She has an Austrian passport!" This was news to him, too, but he seemed to be exceedingly happy about it. He leapt up, passport in hand, and walked resolutely out the door. I was alone with the other men and again felt the menace of their stares which glided up my bare legs, pulled at my clothes like greedy hands, and undressed me. I was suffocating in the heaviness of the room; I crossed my arms again, defensively, and held the collar of my blouse closed. But my knees were bare, and I had nothing with which to cover them except my disdain. So I let go of my collar and scowled into their faces, making myself heavy and calm.

They were quiet now and studied me like an exotic animal caught in a trap. They passed the stringed instrument around the room, from hand to hand, and finally gave it to me, gesturing for me to play. I shook my head and passed the instrument on to the student. Yassin picked up a rusty dagger that had been lying on a brass table in the corner, took it out of its sheath, and passed that around like the instrument. "Feel how sharp it is," he said in Hebrew, running his thumb along the blade and grinning at me intimately, as if he knew all about me and was claiming me as his booty. With great nonchalance, he leaned over, reached under my collar and pulled out my silver Star of David. He smiled and yanked my necklace, a hard, quick jerk; the chain cut into my skin but didn't break. Then he let go.

The men looked at me as if they were awaiting the results of their novel experiments. I was determined not to show fear, not even when Sa'id stepped behind me, put his hand on my shoulder, and pulled an object out of his pants pocket which I couldn't recognize out of the corner of my eye. Without turning my head I tried to see what he had in his hand—a handkerchief, a piece of rope, a crumpled gray rag? Would he put it around my neck, blindfold me, or gag me? He fumbled with it and the others watched him full of suspense. He held my shoulder in a viselike grip. The only sound in the room was a steady ticking like a wristwatch. I knew this fear but I couldn't remember where from. Later, I felt the same terror in a nightmare in which a dark animal was lying in wait. Suddenly it leaped out at me and I screamed and screamed but couldn't produce a sound.

The student let go of my shoulder and put his hand over my mouth and nose. I couldn't recognize the smell on his hand but then Sivan, my treacherous savior, appeared at the door.

"Let's go," he said, standing at the door and addressing me. He made a gesture with his hand, flicking away the man standing behind me. Sa'id protested but their exchange was brief. Yassin and the dark man stood up and our host allowed us to pass him in the hallway, one by one. What was it that I saw in his eyes? He seemed to have something to say to me but then thought better of it. We paused for a second and held each other's gaze as if we'd been in silent conversation.

Outside, the dark man got back into the driver's seat; the car would be stoned if I took the wheel, Sivan explained. A different stranger appeared out of the darkness, got into the car, and sat in the back between me and Sivan. No one said a word. He pressed up hard against me. I squeezed into the corner of the seat but he kept pushing and I felt his warm body all the way from my calf to my shoulder, a heavy mass I struggled against for the length of the journey. Until the roadblock appeared in the headlights, and then I forgot him.

Wooden barrels obstructed our path as they do on every West Bank road and the soldiers, their rifles at the ready, left no doubt that they'd force us to stop. But the man behind the wheel turned off the headlights and raced past them into the blackness of the unlit road beyond. We were a dark projectile hurtling into nothing. No one dared turn around and not a word was spoken, except for Yassin's mumbled instructions to the driver, until we could see the outlines of houses on the horizon. A ghost town, black and eerie, a village whose name I never learned, a few black walls we glided along in silence.

Before he stopped, the dark man turned the headlight back on. Then we came to a halt in front of a white wall and changed places. Sivan told me the lie about the missing driver's licenses, then we were silent again, except for the directions he gave me as I drove. Dazed, and without a clear thought in my head, I drove along a straight road back to Jerusalem. I couldn't form a coherent sentence, as if my mind were stuck back in Ramallah and had given up any desire to escape. As we entered Jerusalem the four men in the car rolled down the windows and whistled at women in other cars. I was struggling to connect thought and sensation, and for a while I was afraid I'd lost my mind.

They had me stop at the Lion's Gate, where they got out and disappeared without explanation. "Wait here," Sivan said, and I stared dully ahead. I wasn't in the least worried that something might happen to me in East Jerusalem, in the middle of the night, in an Israeli car. I tried to fight my numbness to arrive at some clarity, but gave up in dismay. Blank, in a state of limbo, feeling neither suspicion nor impatience, I waited for Sivan to return. But he didn't come back alone. Both Yassin and the dark man climbed back into the car. Only the stranger, whom I wouldn't recognize if I saw him again, had been swallowed up as suddenly as he'd appeared.

At the Jaffa Gate, the other two climbed out, but the dark man planted a kiss on my mouth, moist and vulgar. They spoke to Sivan before they departed and he seemed to be haggling for time, pointing to their watches. There was un ugly tone to their voices.

"Let's go," Sivan urged.

But Yassin wouldn't let go of the door handle. Hatred seemed to have sprung up between the men, splitting them apart. They were arguing about me, I'm sure. "How much time do you need to fuck her?" Was that what they were saying?

"Let's go," Sivan pleaded and I drove off so rapidly that Yassin's hand was wrenched from the door handle

We stopped at the approach to the Zion Gate. Now that it was dark and quiet all around Sivan turned to me as though nothing had happened that required an explanation. Before I could ask a question, he embraced me. He kissed me the way he had when we first went to the Mount of Olives, tenderly, gratefully, and relieved.

"What were you planning to do with me in Ramallah?" I asked, freeing myself from his hold.

But he closed my mouth again with kisses.

"Tomorrow," he said, "now I have to go, I promised them."

I drove back to the hotel alone. According to the clock in the lobby, it was two in the morning.

$\mathcal{A}$ monotone birdsong woke me. I stepped outside my room above the Dead Sea. To the east, a bright shimmer touched the peaks of the Jordanian mountains. The lamps along the kibbutz fence faded quickly while the light over the sea scattered a million sparkling splinters in the water. Their dazzle chased me back into the darkness of my room.

An empty day lay ahead. I had no idea how to fill it but I knew I couldn't get through the long day on my own. I didn't want to stay in my room until the sun consumed the last of the shadows and made a prisoner of me in the kibbutz. By the time I went over to the dining room, the day was already weary and torpid from too much sun, and the sea lay heavy as if it had never been touched by a breath of air. Only the mountain goats leapt and played on the slopes, two kibbutzniks were washing a jeep, carefully, deliberately, and the chug of a generator drowned out the desert silence.

The dining hall was empty but there were still a few slices of tomato and cucumber left in the metal dishes, some bread and some cheese. A young Russian interrupted his cleanup duties to sit down with me. He wanted to know if I was a new immigrant too, since my Hebrew seemed to be as bad as his. He was discouraged and depressed, he told me, this wasn't the life he'd imagined. He didn't know how he'd landed here in the desert. It wasn't so much different from Siberia, well, maybe not quite as bad. After all, they had trips every week, and Jerusalem wasn't all that far away, theoretically. No, he didn't really want to complain, it's only that while he studied engineering in Moscow he'd never dreamed that he'd find himself washing floors and clearing breakfast tables.

But what can you do? He raised his hands and shoulders in a gesture of resigned futility.

His name was Chaim, and he'd concentrated on desert irrigation before he'd ever seen a desert and found out that he couldn't live in such a place, that he needed the city, and music. He displayed an almost manic enthusiasm for classical music. He sang melodies and arias for me, with much waving of his hands and stamping of his feet. Language didn't matter, we didn't need language to talk about music, and we both burst into laughter because suddenly it all seemed so grotesque, the way we were yelling out the names of symphonies and humming themes to each other, two strangers in an empty dining hall on a mountaintop in the desert.

And the whole time I was trying to place who he reminded me of. Was it Gilbert? No, it was a woman's face: the slanting gray eyes, the cheekbones, the small round chin, there was something very familiar in the face, but it wasn't until he began to talk about his family and their tragic story of loss, that I knew: his was the face in the portrait, Martha's face.

As he told me about friends and family left behind in Russia, I told him about Martha, whom I'd almost forgotten over the past few weeks, an infidelity I sought to offset by telling her story now. But the other reason I poured out the whole thing to this stranger was my fear of spending an entire day alone in the heat and isolation. I held onto the Russian engineer to ward off the profound fatigue waiting to engulf me outside in the blazing sun. I wanted to distract it, trick it with a frantic cheerfulness.

"I had an aunt who disappeared without a trace at the beginning of the war," I told him. "Actually, she wasn't really an aunt, she was a cousin of my grandmother, but about seven or eight years younger. They were like sisters. There was a special closeness between them—they grew up together and the two families always spent holidays together." It was so easy to invent Martha's story, I wasn't aware of making anything up—it must have been that way, yes, that's exactly how it was. I could see her in front of me, her hair the color of dark beer and her slender figure extravagantly dressed in avant-garde fashions. "You look a little like her," I confessed to Chaim, and blushed.

"How old was she?" he wanted to know.

I counted. "She would have been seventy-nine now. I don't know how long she lived."

"There are lists of people deported to the camps," Chaim said. "It's not that difficult to find out."

"I've always been looking for someone who's still alive, in America with my great uncle's daughters, in England, in Israel."

"Never in Yad Vashem?"

"I hadn't given up."

"In the meantime, she could have died of any one of a hundred natural causes, assuming she survived, but she probably didn't," Chaim concluded.

Suddenly, I didn't want to talk about Martha. Chaim's rational deliberations hurt; they annoyed me. What right did he have to rob me of my hope?

When the morning heat became unbearable I drove with him to Ein Gedi, but he was less interested in the scenery than in the piano sonata by Beethoven on the radio. The music was at odds with the desert vista and the car radio crackled and stuttered. Between intervals of silence we sat under tamarisk trees, our feet dangling in the cool water. Our conversation circled around missing people, lost people, and people long dead, even though he was able to tell funny stories about them that made me laugh.

"One branch of the family emigrated to America at the beginning of the century," he told me, "but they had problems at the Russian border and one of the aunts was forced to sleep with a soldier so the others could leave. She had to stay behind and no one ever heard from her again. She was a wonderful, strong woman, by all accounts. Her son, Gedalia, was twelve years old at the time, and after that night he never grew another inch."

I told him about Aunt Wilma, no longer feeling embarrassed by her story. Gradually, we came to know each other's families, the crazy ones and the eccentrics. Maybe we were both talking to fill the silence. Finally, we grew quiet and, lost in our thoughts, stared at the waterfall, cascading like a translucent veil into a gravel basin.

Most tourists head straight for the main waterfall and I could hear their voices in the distance. The torrent deepened our silence and we were quiet longer than we had been speaking. As evening approached, we drove back to the kibbutz.

"That was wonderful," Chaim said, when we got back to the dining hall. "Thank you for taking me with you. You know, I'm ashamed to admit it, but I'm homesick for Moscow. I just can't find a way to start a new life here." He got out and went back to the kitchen without turning around.

As I went to the television room, I was unexpectedly seized by anxiety. I thought I'd shed the fear in the desert. The television stood in the corner and red plastic chairs were casually arranged in front of it. The announcer, dressed in sickly, unnatural colors, was reading the weather report and forecast the searing heat of a *hamsin* and possible sandstorms. No one turned to look at me as I entered the room, but one man sitting in the corner glanced my way every once in a while, with a peculiar look on his face. I didn't know what to make of it—he seemed to be consulting a mental image and checking me off against it. Is this the woman? So that's what she looks like.

I sat down at the other end of the room and looked over his way from time to time, but then our eyes locked and we both quickly turned away. Finally, he'd seen enough and left the room.

Had they hooked up with me again? But why would they let

me get this far in the first place? Just because I'd driven to the desert?

And suddenly they all had this look in their eyes, as if they knew me and were there to find out more—the friendly girl in reception and the two young men with backpacks and exhausted faces who stopped at the door for a while. Furtive glances full of mistrust and expectation darted around the room. One couple got up and left, mumbling some sort of salutation as they went. I felt like one of the ten most wanted, my face on posters everywhere, and considered turning myself in out of decency, just to put an end to this game of hide and seek. Instead I stole out of the room like a thief in the night. By now all the people watching television had probably turned away from the newscaster to get a look at me. Maybe they'd moved to the window to watch my retreat.

My guess was that there was only one man on my trail. A professional undoubtedly, and careful, so that I'd never suspect him. Chaim? Or the receptionist? This man knew my habits and what I did when I was alone, he'd even seen me making love. He'd certainly rummaged through my pockets and sniffed at my underwear. He knew my thoughts, how I imagined scenarios sure to bring Sivan to my side. He also knew how frightened I was, how I dreaded the moment he'd step out of the shadows and show his face, but how I longed for it at the same time. I needed him nearby—he gave my life shape and purpose. Much of what I did was to please him.

On the other hand, if he really knew me so well he'd have given up the chase long ago, because he'd know I was simply desperate and confused, wandering around in the dark wanting to know who'd been using me. Once the spy shows himself, I thought, maybe we can work together since we're searching for the same thing—the truth. I'd put myself entirely at his service and even show him Sivan's picture. I wouldn't be ashamed—he knew my secrets after all. Not a single piece of evidence would I hold back, not even the most negligible detail and he'd have to listen because that's what he's paid to do.

I'd go over to the other side willingly and finally free myself from this bitter love, maybe even work myself into such a rage it would turn to hate. Just give me the chance to talk myself back to freedom.

My thoughts swirled. No one version of the night in Ramallah had led me out of my maze and all of them pointed to catastrophe.

I needed him, my spy, to finally set things straight and pluck out the one definite truth from among the many possibilities that coexisted in my poor aching brain even as they contradicted each other. This is how it is in the Orient, Nurit would say, but I didn't believe her. I wanted only to free myself from this incomprehensible piece of my past before it killed me, even if it meant losing the last, best parts of Sivan.

"Listen," I told my spy, "here is how he looked. You have to put his image with our other artifacts. How can we achieve total clarity if we don't weigh all the evidence? Here's his thick dark hair curling behind his ears. Here's the scar above his eye, his honey-dipped skin, his teasing fingers. Take them, take them, everything, you have to tremble with desire as I do and then maybe you'll tell me: was he the greatest love or the greatest fraud?

It was seven-thirty when I left the television room. Again the moon had thrown down a path of silvery lights between two hostile shores, but it seemed to end in a broad puddle on the Jordanian coast. The bunkers and trenches at the border were touched by moonlight and their metallic sheen transformed the cacti into shiny sculptures. A scorpion crawled out from under the stone I was sitting on and gleamed in the light for a moment. The mountain peak had turned inhospitable and threatening, and the flat sheet of sea below gave me a hollow feeling of defeat, like the silence that had risen up between me and Chaim in the car. It wasn't antipathy nor even impatience, just the weary certainty that I'd had enough.

That's how it ended with Gilbert at the kibbutz in Ashkelon. First the need, every morning, to stop time and hold off the end. Then without the slightest sense of transition, the way night falls over the desert, fatigue and the days became long and draining. And suddenly, for no palpable reason, we'd had our fill and were impatient to be on the first ship out of Haifa. Just for a month or two, we'd said at the kibbutz. We'll be back for the avocado harvest. Just a short vacation in Greece before it gets too cold to sleep outside. We lay next to one another in our sleeping bags under the skies, but I buried my face in my elbow, not wanting to see either the stars or the vanishing coastline. I'd had enough.

"This divine night sky!" I heard a gushing female voice but remained resolutely stretched out on deck with my back to the night, lulled by the ship's gentle roll. When I thought that Gilbert was asleep I ate handfuls of raisins and almonds that I'd found in the kibbutz storeroom.

I was overcome by animosity toward Gilbert, a repulsion which bordered on disgust and for which there was no explanation.

"Hey, shrimp," he said, awake. "Aren't you going to give me some of those?"

"No." I rolled myself up tightly inside my sleeping bag and lay still.

Gilbert stroked my head. "Are you okay?" he asked. And because I didn't answer or move, he sang softly and went on stroking my hair. But I didn't want him any more; I wanted to move on, on and on, and away from him.

We split up in Greece, in front of the youth hostel. The summer heat felt old and stale in the narrow whitewashed streets. By winter I was already regretting my decision. Gilbert had not gone back to the kibbutz either, and no one there had a forwarding address. Fifteen years later, he sent a letter to my father's address. His handwriting hadn't changed. He was living on Long Island, he reported. He was now a rabbi, just what he'd always wanted. I sent him a detailed eight-page status report and indicated that I might visit him in New York. I wondered how he looked with short hair, and did he remember laying naked in the Ashkelon dunes?

Six weeks later, I received a letter which discouraged such intimacies. The past was one thing, those were youthful pranks. But we could still correspond, we'd always had so much to talk about.

I didn't answer the letter, nor the greetings he sent for the New Year or on Passover. I didn't want to taint my memories with mature banalities. I could do without his letters and cards, preferring to hold firmly to images that had faded with the years, the way he sat on the only chair in our room bent over his guitar while I was trying to sleep, his hair falling over his face and his back. The way he plowed the sand path between the barracks with his big, dirty feet. The way the shade of plane trees in the Philistine ruins speckled his tanned body. The way he spread his fingers when he poured hot peppermint tea into a glass, and the way he took me in his arms, shutting out everything that troubled me.

When I moved to New York, I didn't call him.

On my second day in the desert I was awakened early. Not by the bird sitting in the cacti singing the only two notes he knew, but by a dream. I had discovered him, Sivan, in the bushes on the slope leading up to Mount Zion. We sat on the wall, cradling each other's face with our hands, as if we had just found a precious object lost long ago. In my dream I wondered whether I was allowed to do that to my enemy. I opened my eyes and tasted bitter loss on my tongue.

Pale stars hung over the lemon yellow glow spreading on the horizon. By the time I walked out the door with my suitcase, the sun was breaking above the mountains. It wasn't a good morning to spend in the desert but I wanted to be alone. On the slopes, the scree glowed like coals in the first light, hot and sulfurous, chasing the last blue night shadows away from the gorges. The sea was a gray haze evaporating into the sky.

Down on the coastal road, I had two options: south, deeper into the desert, or north to Jericho, to the West Bank and back to Jerusalem. For Sivan, Ein Gedi had marked the last outpost between him and the land of the Jews.

"Shall we keep going?" I'd asked. It was our first afternoon with the rental car and our enthusiasm for driving was still fresh.

"Where to?"

"Masada, maybe Arad."

"No, let's stick with the beach."

At Ein Gedi we were both tourists in neutral territory, and I caught a glimpse of all the things we could have done together were it not for the unspoken words dividing us. We could have swum in the Mediterranean at Caesarea or Acre and watched the breakers crashing into the Wall of the Crusaders, gouging out its ancient foundations and retreating in fountains of sparkling spray. He could have taken me to the souk in Hebron and introduced me to the stall-keepers as we bought olives and apricots and spices. We could have been free of shame and secrecy and the doubt that flooded my thoughts whenever we parted, Sivan turning east while I went west.

I was alone in the desert with Sivan's map in my head: south across his imaginary border to Sedom and Arad, Beersheba and Ashkelon, to my kibbutz, which I'd been avoiding for twenty years; north to the West Bank and Jerusalem. Shimmering waves of heat pounded the windshield, skimming over the endless ribbon of asphalt, blurring the road's edge and veiling the mountains. And silence. No cicadas, no rustling, no waves crashing in from the sea, not even the faintest flicker of breeze in the merciless hot air. And no shade anywhere, not even for the smallest insects.

Great rocks squatted motionless in the heavy silence and fields of scree lay petrified in the scorched valleys. The battered landscape, washed by great waves of heat day after day, held its breath until the first liberating shade of late afternoon. Outlined with ridges cut by the wind, the desert's cratered horizon was encrusted in salt and bleached white as ancient bones. But rifts in the surface ran down to the seething center of the earth and at night the wind carved towns in the desert floor, chiseled cathedrals in the dunes, and erected walls of sand that were razed by morning.

I never reached Arad. The heat raged in my head and the yellow glimmering sun danced before my eyes. Sand dunes wandered from one side of the road to the other, blocking my path, and a shimmering sea swallowed up the road ahead. Swaying palms in the distance stayed just beyond my reach and dancing shafts of sand never touched the ground. Silence. Not a breath of air. Suddenly I was overcome by dread. Nothing moved, yet nothing stood in one place. The ossified landscape had been seized by playfulness; it trembled and quivered and threatened to bury my car under sand and stone. Gas pedal to the floor, I drove back to Ein Gedi, hurtling out of a deadly landscape where I'd hoped to find consolation or insight or freedom from the compulsion to remember.

Past Ein Gedi I drove straight through to Jericho without stopping. The bathers on the beach, the overflowing parking lot, the pilgrims pouring out of tour buses, the hitchhikers trudging up to the youth hostel—everything overwhelmed me. The transition was too abrupt. The sea, exhausted and pale, followed me on my right, the dry brush trudged along on my left like a dusty herd of hedgehogs. Far away on the horizon the bluish gray desert ridges swayed like the backs of elephants.

I turned off toward the center of Jericho and passed the dark shops of the main street, not the least concerned about who might be watching me. At a kiosk I bought warm pita bread and goat cheese and looked for a place to sit, faint from hunger and fear. In the shade of a lush tree with fiery blossom, I found a small table and chair, both a little shaky and sticky. Several old men sat near me playing a board game.

The kiosk owner brought me strong Turkish coffee. In the end, life was simple—eating, drinking, feeling the exhaustion and trembling in my limbs give way to a tired indifference. I looked at the dismal shacks and fruit stands on the sidewalk, the women carrying baskets atop their long dark robes and white veils, the men hauling brightly colored plastic bags—a weekday in the village, its rhythm slow and deliberate. So slow that evening could come and there would still be time enough to make a decision.

Teenagers cycled along the broken streets, coming to a halt next to my car, an alien object with its Israeli plates. Someone pointed at me, uncertain; someone else crossed from the other side of the street, eyeing me. Passersby stopped, shopkeepers stood in their doorways. My car disturbed the equilibrium. People were speculating, talking, gesticulating, but I was isolated in the silence of incomprehension. I paid for the food, smiled, and crossed to my car, composed but watchful, ready to flee. I pulled out of the parking spot very carefully, taking care not to graze another car or a crate, not to cause the slightest annoyance. I kept my face affable and indifferent and my eyes fixed ahead, feeling the gazes I dared not return and remembering the warnings of smashed windshields, Molotov cocktails, slit tires.

This is my last trip, I thought, as I drove from the Jordan basin up into the mountains in the yellow light of a late afternoon. Black shadows slid over the slopes, torn Beduin tents flapped in a gentle breeze, and black dots of sheep wandered in the gray-green thorn bushes. My last evening in the desert.

In the end, we parted as enemies. That's the way Sivan wanted it.

I'd intended to visit Jaffa, but that morning, after we left the hotel, I just didn't feel like it. Alone, I'd usually let the hours pass, watching from the window as they expanded endlessly, filling up with emptiness, until it was time to meet Sivan again early in the evening.

At the end, I wanted to tell him all about myself. Clearly we both had pasts and there was no longer any point to secrecy. But there was no appropriate moment for my stories, which weren't really of interest to anyone but myself. There was no place for them in this city. Sivan and I inhabited our roles, we had no means to discard them.

When I got to our meeting place, the sidewalk was empty. I sat on Sivan's concrete bollard, and it forced me to sit exactly as he did, upper body pushed slightly forward, knees spread apart. Without warning he was standing behind me, so close that I could smell his scent and feel his warmth with my body.

"I've been standing behind you for a while," he said. "Sometimes I've walked behind you and you never even noticed."

He often made a game of surprising me.

"Did you go to Jaffa?" he asked.

"No, I didn't feel like it."

He looked at me suspiciously. "You've got someone else."

"I was in my hotel all morning by myself."

"You're lying." Sivan was so sure that I didn't deny it.

We went to Independence Park. It was late afternoon and there were many young couples with small children camping in the shade of the tall trees.

"Let's go somewhere else," I suggested, "there's no place for us here."

But Sivan wanted to be with people, be protected by the

crowds, perhaps. The pimp from the previous day was sitting near a clump of bushes. When I recognized him, he responded with the grin of a conspirator. Once we sat down he moved closer until he was within earshot, no more than five meters away.

Sivan lit two cigarettes and offered me one, holding the burning end to my lips for a brief moment before turning it around, a trace of cruelty in his eyes.

"I don't want it," I said.

We sat quietly for a long time. I caressed his stubbly cheek gently.

"Are you growing a beard?" I asked.

He looked right past me.

"Stay here," he begged.

"You know I can't. I have a plane to catch and a job. My vacation is over."

"There are ways to make you stay," he said.

"Like what?"

"Your passport could get lost."

I laughed but Sivan stood up and took my bag, which had been lying on the ground next to us, hung it over his shoulder, and walked away without turning around to look at me. The pimp moved a little closer. I decided to ignore Sivan's game and stay put. Half an hour later he showed up again, approaching from the opposite direction, with the bag still slung over his shoulder. Nothing was missing, not even the money. I counted it later at the hotel.

He sat down next to me, smoked another cigarette, and looked over the bushes into the distance. The beard made his face older and harder, impenetrable.

"What's wrong?" I asked.

"I don't want you to leave," he said harshly.

I leaned over to kiss him as he threw himself down to the ground, burying his face in his elbow, and refused to look up at me.

I gently stroked his short hair, which took on a bluish tint in the sun.

When he finally turned around, his face was wet.

"Do you wish you had never met me?" I asked.

He nodded. "And you?"

"Not me, never."

He held my neck in his hand and stared at me, his eyes black. "Stay here," he said calmly, "or I'll kill you."

"You're crazy."

Sivan squeezed my neck with both hands, choking me there on the grass with all the people around, and I thought my head would burst. Then he let go and watched calmly as I gasped for air. I looked around but only the pimp was looking at us.

Sivan said a few words. "Repeat them after me." It sounded like Arabic.

"What do they mean?"

"It's Armenian. Please say it, I want to hear it from you."

I repeated the words, listening to the tone in an attempt to understand what I'd just said.

"Say it again," he asked.

"Only if you tell me what it means."

He shook his head. Every question of mine met with silence.

"Now you're just wrecking everything out of spite," I said. "I'm leaving. You're not going to destroy my memories, too."

Sivan followed, nudging me in the direction of Mamilla

Cemetery. I reached for his hand but he pinched my arm every time I got close to him.

"You're hurting me, I've had enough." I looked behind and saw a young man behind us. He looked familiar and in his eyes I thought I could read the unyielding hate of silent curses.

Sivan responded with a desperately tender embrace and I stayed by his side. The young man passed us and Sivan tried to keep up with him, step for step. He began taking giant strides, and abruptly turned down an alleyway I didn't know.

"What's going on?" I called after him.

"Something happened."

"What?"

"Nothing you'd understand."

"Can't you tell me anyway?"

"Shut up," he yelled. As Sivan turned around to make sure no one had heard, a black-hatted Hasid overtook us. I couldn't tell whether he'd been paying attention to us.

A long way off, past Yemin Moshe, past Hebron Street, in Hinnom Valley, among the acacia and agave, we found an isolated clearing. A white moon hung over Mount Zion, a perfect round cloud.

"Let's stay together," Sivan started in again. "We could find a way if you really wanted to."

"How?" I asked impatiently. "We know nothing about each other. You avoid every question I ask, and you don't know anything about me either."

"I saw your passport," he said. "I know how old you are and what your name is, where you live, where you were born. I know you're divorced—"

"That's not what I mean," I interrupted. "There are all the

things we're still hiding from each other. You say you love me but you don't know me. I don't know what you see when you look at me. What do you think? That I'm an easy tourist? Some Jewish woman you can screw? Someone you didn't mean to fall in love with? What?"

"I know you think you're very special," he said coolly. "You talk about your life and your successes over there in New York, but really you're like a child, and not a particularly smart one. You think you're better than me just because you're Jewish. You know what you are? Zero, nothing. I saw it from the very beginning. You're so scared someone's going to find out the truth about you. All this song and dance about yourself and you're blind really. But none of that bothers me. I love you anyway."

"That's not enough," I started, but a deep exhaustion drained all sense from the rest of my sentence. There was nothing left to say. My words were hollow. We had reached our last silence.

I got up first. We walked back to Yemin Moshe, careful not to touch. There was no hate between us but we were enemies, sundered by helpless grief. Our enmity was our silence, and at its center our love lay wounded in the stillness.

"There's one thing I'd like to know," Sivan said. "Why did you kiss me that evening when we met?"

"Because I liked you and trusted you."

"Because you liked me? That's all?"

"Why? What else?"

We crossed King Solomon Street and headed up to Jaffa Road, almost running, as if we could hardly wait to say good-bye. We slowed down at my bus stop where an old man had been stabbed a few weeks earlier by a Palestinian from the West Bank.

Sivan had refused to call him a terrorist. The old man had survived a death camp.

"You can take any bus along this route," Sivan said.

"I'll wait for the number twenty."

We stood facing each other but Sivan avoided my eyes. He looked over my shoulder, watching for the bus. It had grown cold and I shivered as I always do when the damp night settles on Jerusalem. The number twenty approached from the Jaffa Gate and Sivan embraced me, kissing me once hard, pressing all his unspoken words into his seal. Then I climbed in, took my seat, and looked down directly into his solemn eyes.

V

The expressways around Jerusalem have always confused me. They resemble nothing so much as a diversionary maneuver designed to route me out of the city down into the desert or the coastal plain. It wasn't until I hit a traffic jam moving at a snail's pace that I knew I was on the right road.

"Don't get lost in East Jerusalem," the young woman at the rental agency had said.

"I've been there before, it's fine," I protested.

"Sure, nine times out of ten it's fine, and then something happens."

The Old City's northern flank loomed on my right and I felt a happy sense of reunion. The street narrowed, the crates of fruit and vegetables stacked in the gutters were near enough to touch; children balanced baskets and trays on their heads, women held their veils tight beneath their chins, and men propped up doorframes, smoking. No one turned my way, no one looked at my license plate, but my eyes resumed their search when I saw the Damascus Gate ahead. Where else would I find him if not in East Jerusalem? And why not here, why not by chance, the way I'd first met him? And if he were to step out in front of my car, by chance, what could I do but call out and watch as he walked by?

It was still the Sabbath. The oleander trees were radiant white and a wine-colored canopy of sky lay over West Jerusalem. The streets in the west were serenely quiet. Occasionally a car would go by but no buses, and the sidewalks were swept clean. I drove though the city center and into the hills on the other side, past Mount Herzl, and through a housing development which lay hushed in the evening sun.

I knew Channa-Frieda would be at home on a Saturday afternoon. She hardly ever leaves Jerusalem now, not even her house.

"Where have you been?" she asked at the door.

"In the desert."

"Not in East Jerusalem?" she said.

"Actually I just drove through it."

"I thought you'd left already," she got straight to the point.

"I stayed on and now my ticket's expired."

"There's a man in this somewhere, isn't there?"

"Yes and no, it's complicated."

"Tell me later, have a little something to eat first."

I took my usual seat on her low sofa. One side of the art nouveau desk had a crack I hadn't noticed before.

"It's the climate," she said, "the damp winters and the dry heat in summer. There's no one left to repair these old things, the skilled carpenters are dying off."

Channa seemed depressed and uncommunicative.

"The heat is getting to me," she explained, and after a long pause, "the death notices, too. A friend from Germany, a survivor. He wrote poems in German and Hebrew, he could never decide which language he really felt at home in but he was alive, even happy. He'd remarried and had more children after losing his first family over there. So now he killed himself."

Her own husband died fifteen years ago and her children live in Europe and America. They have long-distance telephone conversations and visit her from time to time. Sometimes they all meet up in Italy or Switzerland.

"I won't make any new friends," she said. "I've given up making close friendships. It's too painful otherwise, losing people. But I'm not always so successful and then it hurts anyway."

She brought the coffee in from the kitchen weaving slightly before she caught hold of the door frame.

"I feel a little dizzy today, it's been that way all day." She waved away my concern. "No, no, no, stay where you are. We're not going to any doctor or hospital. You learn to live with it when you get old. You just go kaput, piece by piece."

She agreed to take her blood pressure but stopped when the gauge reached two hundred. "I don't need to know so exactly," she said.

After supper we went to Channa's small bedroom to watch the evening news on television, a ritual she never missed.

"When the news is finished you tell me why you're still here," she said, her voice mixing with the gruff tones of the announcer. ". . . undercover army unit found weapons cache . . . exchange of fire . . . four dead in Jenin, one soldier, three residents of the territories . . ." My Hebrew was always too weak to follow the news.

The face of a young Israeli with laughing eyes and a mocking smile filled the screen. "Left a wife and two small children,"

Channa repeated, "will be buried tomorrow on Mount Herzl." Then came coarse-grained photos from the West Bank, a grimy stairwell, a wall splattered with blood. The three Palestinians were not named.

"Every day," Channa said, "a war with no end."

". . . riot in Gaza," the television went on. ". . . six casualties . . ." Pictures of raised fists and furious faces. News about America and Europe followed, then the weather forecast.

We said good night. I climbed the stairs to the guest room and stood in the darkness of the open window, looking down at the road from Ein Kerem shimmering in the moonlight. More dead every day. How do they announce their dead on the other side, in Jenin and Jericho? The men without names have wives, children, parents. Over there, in Jenin and Jericho, they're not terrorists but freedom fighters, martyrs.

Almost a whole month had passed since Sivan and I drove through the desert night for the last time. Beduin fires were burning on the mountains and in the distant villages dogs howled like jackals, goading each other on.

"Rosh Hodesh," I said, "the new Jewish month." I'd been reminded of the ancient Jewish practice of marking time with a fire in the mountains.

"What are you talking about?" Sivan asked roughly. "And why are you speaking Hebrew all of a sudden?"

At the most trivial of provocations hatred would rise from him like a scent, even after moments of intimacy. That was the evening when our brakes failed.

The next morning I left Channa's and took the car back to Keren Hayesod Street. After that I was free to wander. But I went to the windmill at Yemin Moshe as if pulled by a string, compelled like an addict who has no control over her decisions. At the first sight of the Old City walls and David's Tower I drew a breath of relief.

I crossed Hinnom Valley. There was a herd of sheep grazing among the mulberry trees. A child was driving black and white sheep over the stony slopes of Mount Zion. The air was clear and flooded with light. A morning fragrance of rosemary and lavender wafted down from the valley, and two lovers were stretched out beneath an olive tree.

As I neared the Jaffa Gate I hit a thick wall of tension. Teenagers were hanging out as usual, squatting like chickens on the pilings and chains, but the souk was cold and gloomy, stripped of its wares—the copper pots, marbled backgammon sets, and embroidered Beduin robes. The shops' metal shutters were pulled down, showing the faint graffiti beneath a hurried coat of whitewash. A few old men were sitting silently on low stools in doorways, waiting. The Old City was stone-still with dread. A green police van with barred windows had stopped before David's Tower.

The Armenian Quarter was deserted; the clatter of my sandals echoed loudly off the paving stones. Two rifles protruded above an archway. Soldiers lay up on the roofs behind hanging bougainvillea and sumac. Two sharp-faced priests rushed past in long habits and black hoods. Habits like that would make a good camouflage, I thought. My stomach in knots, I ran past the Zion Gate into the Jewish Quarter. Which side was I on? I knew too much, too many faces and names. I could identify them and their meeting place in Ramallah. Maybe I could even find it again; why should they trust me? When I got to Chabad Street my steps slowed.

There were more soldiers than usual in the Jewish Quarter.

They stood on corners with their weapons slung over their shoulders but the shops were all open. Like guests at a buffet the tourists meandered from postcard stands to display tables and sat on curbs in the shade of straggling trees or at the café tables that lined the broad plaza. The quarter looked as well-groomed as a barmitzvah boy; only the stubborn issop grew unruly between the cracks in the sidewalk. The Russian musicians were still playing "Jerusalem the Golden" on their violins and a few soldiers watched them while eating falafel. Here the soldiers were not intruders and did not disturb anyone, they could have been tourists or young recruits on an outing.

Still, I was edgy. I heard whispers through the thick walls and across the fine cracks in the street. I was waiting for a jolt, a big blast, ready even to set it off—anything to end the uncertainty. Israelis might be more even-keeled, have the patience to wait, but I was worn down by weeks of fantasies. I longed for clarity, no matter how cruel.

On the broad steps to the Western Wall, I asked Jodie why so many soldiers were stationed in the streets. She was just about to scare off a tourist who was hanging around too close to her pictures with a camera. "Copyright!" she screamed, and threw herself in front of her work to protect it.

"Did you see that?" she yelled. "They're copying my art."

"What's going on in the souk?" I asked again.

"I don't know," she shrugged. "I never go over there."

"They're on strike and it's only ten in the morning. All the stores are closed."

"I wouldn't know," said Jodie. "It's the PLO or something."

Two blocks away they're on strike, hurling rocks and spraying the walls with their anger, but Jodie has to guard her work while undaunted, she waits for the coming of the Messiah.

I bought a copy of *The Jerusalem Post* on my way to the Cardo and was reminded of Adam. I hadn't seen him for a while. The first time we met I was carrying *The Jerusalem Post*. "Are you a journalist?" he asked.

"Why? Do you have an interesting story?"

"They burned a car on Nablus Street and someone threw a Molotov cocktail into the terrace of the Har Zion Hotel. Then the police detonated a bag full of explosives at the Central Bus Station. All this in one day."

"That's nothing new. I read it in the paper."

"Okay, so it's not new but that's the way it is here."

The shoot-out in Jenin was buried two or three pages back. I couldn't focus on the jumping headline and the text hazed over so my eyes slid to the pictures. I looked at Sivan's startled face and couldn't comprehend how his passport photo had made its way into the newspaper. Four dead in Jenin. The young Israeli soldier from the television to be buried on Mount Herzl. An unfamiliar bearded man with squinting eyes. Sivan must be dead. I'm not sure that comprehension came, even after a few hours. Mostly, I felt wonder, almost a trace of joy to see the face I missed so much, to have news, even from a newspaper.

The Cardo was dark, blanketed with a clammy chill. Anahita was wearing her usual blue dress and was surrounded by her mirrors and jewelry.

"What's going on in the souk?"

"Maybe it's got something to do with Jenin," she said. "They say that two or three of them got away and one might be from East Jerusalem."

"Did you know any of them?"

"Why are you asking me? How would I know them?" Her face showed a flicker of suspicion.

"Because one of them might have been Armenian."

"That's crazy," she protested.

I handed her the newspaper. "It's him."

Her face slowly cleared with understanding.

"You were with him."

It was not a question but a verdict, delivered with revulsion and disbelief. She turned away and started to rummage in one of her desk drawers, then fiddled with a display of Seder plates, walked past me to the door, and looked up and down the street. I left quietly, without a word of farewell, as two customers turned in the door. I was no longer welcome in Anahita's boutique; I had become a threat she could not afford. When I looked back from the darkness of the Cardo her face was still.

Aimless, I sat on the steps leading up from the Cardo. From time to time I looked at the picture. Perhaps I was mistaken; it could be someone else; then my eyes met Sivan's startled gaze and I knew it was no mistake. It wasn't until several hours later that I read the report and started to fill the sentences with meaning. Now I had a name: he was Sawad Radadeh from East Jerusalem, twenty-four years old.

I still could have been wrong; he might have a doppelgänger. How many times had I thought I'd seen Sivan from my hotel window? But then I wanted him to be alive, desperately. Who is mourning you, Sawad? Your mother, your brother, your wife? Was it your eyes that watched me through the window of the number twenty bus? The images of us engraved in his memory had died with him; and so my memories became doubly precious. Our time together had unraveled, its threads carried off in the wind, a whole world of desires and thoughts and experience, contained in one beloved presence, was spilled, gone. But the Israeli—his jokes and wisdom and years of memories were gone too. How could I allow myself to mourn him, Sivan, Sawad? He belonged to the other side. But the other side had losses, too.

That evening I went to see Nurit in the moshav where she lived, on the southern edge of Jerusalem. It was getting dark and the streets grew broader and less familiar. Soon high-rises gave way to row houses and then to open fields.

Nurit lived alone in a small one-story house with large drafty windows. Not ten meters away, through a mesh wire fence, was a chicken farm. Thousands of mangy hens lay in their cages, separated by long, clean walkways. When Nurit left her kitchen window open the smell of chicken droppings came on the breeze. But her two rooms were a long way from the spartan accommodations of farm life and the smoldering conflicts of the city. Indian miniatures hung on the whitewashed walls, embroidered pillows lay on the floor, and sweet, exotic incense burned in the air.

Nurit wore a red sari over a long black skirt, and her luxuriant hair—even more curly in the evening humidity than in the dry sunlight—was thrown back over her shoulders. She'd prepared a buffet as if she were expecting a large crowd of guests: vine leaves stuffed with rice, tahini, falafel, salads. We ate on the floor resting on her Indian pillows.

"Do you mind if I eat with my fingers?" she asked.

Later she showed me the bedroom and the bath. "I'd like you to move in here when I go to India," she said. "I think you'd be happy here. It's so peaceful and still close to the city. You should stay."

"When are you going?"

"Soon. Ada is going to take over the store. I've never been really happy here," she said. "I always felt that I wasn't good enough. Second best. Like Leah. Can you imagine what it was like for her when Rachel died, knowing Jacob wished she had died instead. You know, it's something I've suffered from since my childhood. I had a brother who was born with heart disease. He was the center of attention, the apple of my parents' eyes, their endless sorrow. I was wild and energetic and always had to be careful around him. I hated him. He died when he was seven. I'll never be free of the guilt and I was no consolation for my parents. I guess it's no surprise that when I started meeting men, I never felt like the first or the best."

"But it isn't just a personal thing. As a child I had a close friend whose grandmother came from Poland. She treated me like a filthy illiterate. I read everything I could about Western thinking, I probably knew more than she did but that didn't make any difference. It meant the end of my friendship. Later I discovered the Orient, it's sensuousness and balance, and that got me into more trouble. I met a Beduin—he carried the desert around with him like an aura. It was amazing. When I was with him I felt there was nothing else in the world, but it was impossible. It wasn't us, it was everyone else; you can't go out with an Arab in Israel. There's just no place where you'll both feel comfortable. You can't go to the movies or to a restaurant or share friends."

A cat outside meowed plaintively.

"I don't know who she belongs to," Nurit said. "I don't want to let her in and get used to me just as I'm leaving."

"When do you want to move in?" she asked.

"I don't know whether the time is right for it."

"You love the city, you feel at home here, what are you waiting for?"

"It's a big step, I can't decide. I'll call you in the next few days." I took the last bus back to the Central Bus Station.

I kept the truth from Nurit right through to the end.

The tension had let up. Sivan was gone. I had learned very little, but it was pointless to go on looking for answers. No one but Sivan knew the truth. It was time to leave. I felt no wiser, only more sober, more alone.

Last days are always chock full of leave taking. I wanted to say good-bye, not just to friends but to the Old City, the walls, the streets, the pedestrian mall, Mount Zion and the Mount of Olives. I wanted to see it all again.

I called Nurit. "I'll be back," I said, "I just don't know when."

"I may not be here then. I do wish you'd stay," she said.

Eli was offended that I hadn't come to see him since the afternoon on Mount Scopus. He hadn't meant to be critical, just to give me a warning. "Do you still want to go to Wadi Kilt?" he said, his voice full of reproach.

"Next time, Eli, the next time I come."

"Why go if you're already talking about coming back?"

Channa is the only person who thinks I should leave for a while. "You're not really here, in any case," she said. "You need to give yourself a little distance otherwise you're in danger of getting the Jerusalem Syndrome, God forbid. You'll be wandering around with ecstasy in your eyes, like those crazy women we heard about in Hebron."

And suddenly I didn't know what to do with my time. I hailed a taxi to the Mount of Olives.

"Absolutely not," the driver said. "I won't drive up there, not even for a thousand dollars."

"Why not?"

"Too dangerous."

I talked him into taking me up to Mount Scopus.

The sun was low on the horizon, its glare still striking the white cubes of the cemetery that lay sprawled down the mountain slope. The city lay still beneath the shimmering haze, ringed by a belt of bright stones under which were buried centuries of the dead. The first shadows of night gathered in the Kidron Valley.

A young man came walking toward me, purposefully, taking long strides. He could show me some beautiful views, he promised. I went a little way with him, to the slope beneath the high walls of Gethsemane, where the onion domes of the Russian Church hovered full and yellow over the pines and cypresses. I rested against the sun-soaked stones, warm, content, like a purring cat.

"I've got some olive oil," the young man said. "It's good for you. May I give you a massage?"

"No," I said brusquely, "I have to go now."

"I'll take you down to the Kidron Valley," he offered.

"No, I'm going to the Hyatt Hotel."

At the edge of the village at Et Tur I hailed a taxi with West Bank plates which brought me to the Lion's Gate. A tremor ran through my body and I felt enervated, as if I had just suffered a bout of fever.

The last of the sun's rays withdrew into the hills on the western side of Jerusalem and twilight lay translucent and gray over the Old City.

"The Jaffa Gate," I said to the unshaven profile of my taxi driver. His eyes were taking my measure in the rearview mirror. Without saying a word, he drove over to the Lion's Gate and would go no farther. He wouldn't leave the eastern part of the city. "Then the Damascus Gate at least," I pleaded, but he was already negotiating through the window with his next passenger.

I strode through the dark, narrow streets of the Muslim Quarter with a steady step, not looking behind me. The shops were closed, the streets damp and dirty, and a thin stream of water ran through the valley formed by the slanting paving stones. I didn't know which way to go, nothing looked familiar. Children in racing carts screamed past me, clattering down the alleyways. Hostility hung in the air as gray turned to pitch-black night. I had never been on this usually bustling street after nightfall.

A group of teenagers started to follow me, keeping pace step by step. I could not shake them. I had lost all sense of direction. I heard the sound of shattering glass, maybe ahead of me, then behind me, and shards of broken glass fell like rain. But I kept walking as if I knew where I was going. Once I turned into what I thought was a familiar street only to reach a dead end. There was no one to ask. To the south, I thought, the Jewish Quarter is south of here. But I ran into walls, stepped into courtyards, and stumbled on broken steps in the black night, the teenage boys just a step behind me.

Rounding a corner, I saw a lone shopkeeper building towers of eggplants and tomatoes. Should I ask for the Western Wall or the Via Dolorosa? No street is neutral and for some sites there are three different names, three different code words according to nationality and religion.

"The Damascus Gate?" I asked, relieved at this saving inspiration. He pointed to the left. "*Shukran,* thank you," I said, one of the few Arabic words I knew.

I stepped through the massive dark walls of the Damascus Gate into the cool night like an escaped prisoner. The city had closed itself to me, it had disguised itself and turned hostile. It was only nine o'clock when I got to the Central Bus Station. I bought two stony hard bagels at a stand and then took the bus to Channa's house.

"Don't say good-bye, don't say anything. I fear nothing as much as I fear leave taking," Channa said.

So I embraced her and waved from my taxi while she stood in the doorway.

"Have a good trip," she called out and quickly turned inside.

I held the city with my eyes right down to the last few houses.

"When you leave," Nurit had asked, "is it like leaving a person you love?"

"Exactly."

"Then you have to stay."

We drove down to the coastal plain. I shared the taxi with a professor heading off on a business trip. He was in good spirits, looking forward to the prospect of spending a month in America.

"How did you like Israel?" he asked.

"It's hard for me to leave."

He glowed with pride of possession and gave me his business card. He was sure I'd be coming back.

Fear had begun to build in my gut, a kind of stage fright before a great event.

"What's your name?" the professor asked.

"Devorah," I said, for the last time.

"Shall we get seats together?" he asked, before he got on line for the security check.

"It might take longer with me," I protested.

"That's okay, I'll wait for you in the cafeteria."

She was very polite, the young woman who asked a few questions about my suitcase, when I had packed it and whether it had been out of my sight. So was the officer who looked at my passport and then asked me to come with him, leading me through the departure lounge and down long corridors into the bright air-conditioned room where I now sit waiting.

I want to especially thank Riva Hocherman
of Metropolitan Books. She has in the deepest
sense translated my book.